Parvenue Throws A Party

A Novel

Wendy Boucher

Hoyden Press, LLC

This is a work of fiction. Names, characters, places, incidents and dialogues are either the product of the author's imagination or, if real, are used fictitiously. Any resemblance to actual persons, living or dead, is entirely coincidental.

Library of Congress Control Number: 2005923988

ISBN 0-9766766-0-5

Designed by Wendy Garrett

Dedicated with love to
Tate and Sophie

Acknowledgments

Parvenue Throws A Party owes a huge thanks to my book club's past and present members: Anne, Annette, Betsy, Betsy, Jeana, Kiki, Leigh, Maribeth, Marie, Mary, Michele, Shannon, and Sharmila for all their support, research contributions and editorial comments. Thanks also to my friends, Katy, Mary and Helen, and my mother, Sandy, who is also an author.

Finally, and most importantly, thanks to my husband, Tate, for his support in every aspect of this project.

Prologue: Tricky Treats
(A junior high low.)

For a moment, I savored the tantalizing notion that everybody inside was waiting for me to arrive before getting the Halloween party started. It was unusually quiet outside Polly Hanson's house considering the twenty or so junior high kids who were supposed to be in the Hanson's game room celebrating the spookiest night of the year. I rang the doorbell twice, clutching the invitation I'd received and brought along as proof that I belonged there. *Would Davey be here too*, I wondered? It was almost a certainty. Davey was definitely a member of Polly's in-crowd around which I revolved like a remote and dependable satellite.

I tucked in a loose strip of bed sheet while I waited for someone to hear me at the door. I was a little late arriving at the party because my mummy costume had been giving me trouble. The costume was my mother's idea. We'd wrapped strips of an old sheet (minus the flower trim) around my body from head to toe and I'd worn a small tee shirt and some polyester shorts underneath. It wasn't the beautiful Princess costume I'd seen at Wendt's Department store. That one had been too expensive. It wasn't a cheerleading outfit. I hadn't made the squad and even I knew that it wasn't cool to wear a cheerleading outfit as a costume in any event. And it wasn't the slightest bit suggestive. Dad would never have permitted it. But with a little luck, I looked cutely mysterious.

Truth be told, I was just overjoyed to have been invited. My old friend from elementary school hadn't forgotten about me after all. I, Janice Darcy, was *cordially* invited! Polly *had* made the seventh grade cheerleading squad. She'd also made a boatload of new friends at Olsen Junior High. Somewhere along the line, Polly had even received that apparently secret phone call that it was time for girls to shave their legs and wear pantyhose. I'd shown up for my first day of junior high wearing knee socks and sneakers with my skirt. *Ugh.* Polly still waved hello to me in the hallways but during the two months since the start of school, our relationship had morphed into something less than equal.

Every day after fourth period, I ran Polly's and my books back to the locker we shared while Polly ran on to the lunchroom to find a table. Polly never went to the locker for me. Not once. And soon enough, there didn't seem to be room for me at the lunch table. *Never mind.* I was on Polly's doorstep about to enter my first ever junior high party and it was quite possible that I, Janice Darcy, could legitimately claim to be Polly's oldest friend at the shebang.

Nobody answered the door so I opened it myself and waved off my mom who was still idling in the driveway. The foyer was dark but I could hear music coming from the back of the large house where the game room was located. Polly and I had held countless slumber parties there. Boy was this different. *Literally*, I giggled to myself. This time there were boys. In fact, I nearly tripped over Jennifer Bean and Scott Mayfield making out near the door.

"Oh, sorry," I mumbled, embarrassed beyond belief. Naturally, I hadn't known that Jennifer and Scott were going steady. I hadn't known that seventh graders kissed. Fortunately, the pair either didn't notice me or didn't care.

I struck my best mummy pose and sidled into the game room. A large group of boys and girls were laughing, dancing, and snacking while a popular song played on the record player. I recognized every one of the twenty kids because not one of them was wearing a costume. Of course at that moment the 45rpm record ended. Looking straight at me, Polly laughed. Then everybody laughed. Even Davey snickered along with the rest of them.

Cutely mysterious? Try unbelievably lame and stupid. With one hand frozen in the air, palm up like an Egyptian drawing, I hung my head down in time to see my dingy mummy costume loosen and sag, exposing polyester gym shorts that were so tight I only ever wore them under short skirts to hide my underwear. Patches of white, baby-flabby skin poked out here and there between the strips of unraveling sheet.

Of course I cried. But before I became totally unglued, Polly came over and apologized. Sort of. "I'm sorry Janice," Polly said, "we decided not to wear costumes." Polly flitted away. "Scott, can you play that record again? It's my new favorite." Giggle, giggle. Polly rejoined the party leaving me to ask the really big question to myself.

Who's "we"?

PART I: DEBUTANTE AT LAST
(I'm really fabulous. Really.)

YOU'RE INVITED
~~YOUR~~

TO: A Get Acquainted Brunch

WHERE: Janice Darcy's House

WHEN: Wednesday, December 10
                            10:00 am

BRING: An Appetite!

RSVP: 555-6871

1. Preparations

My mother-in-law droned on and on, full of excuses. "Elsie's sister, whose daughter is the mother of Jeffrey's classmate from first grade, came down with pneumonia and never left the hospital. So you see, this can't wait. I don't want to make any mistakes with *my* invitations."

Mistakes on invitations? I looked around for one of my invites as Ol' Mule Slides prattled on over the phone about the rate at which her elderly friends were passing away. My mother-in-law (who for some reason wouldn't be caught dead in shoes with a closed heel) had found her excuse not to come to my "little tea." This time it was the pressing need to update the membership list for her women's club.

"So I'm really very sorry, dear," she said, "but I can't make it tomorrow or I'll get behind on the invitations to the Valentine's Day auction. Mustn't invite the dear departed, you know. By the way, why don't you get Jeffrey to proofread your correspondences next time? Bye dear."

I didn't mind that my mother-in-law wasn't coming to the brunch. I'd only invited her out of courtesy and as a distraction for Marcy, my three-and-a-half year old daughter. I was also pretty confident that I'd only invited live guests to the brunch. I strolled into the living room where my husband, Jeff, was spreading another coat of paint on the walls.

"The queen mum can't make it tomorrow. She's got to plan a party for two months from now and apparently the guest list has been shrinking due to broken hips and the like."

"What'd you expect?"

"Nothing, of course. But she says I made a mistake on my invitations."

"Oh yeah, I saw that," he said without glancing down.

"*What*? What mistake?"

Jeff kept working the paintbrush. The details I had so loved about our new house had created a lot of unexpected extra work. With crown moldings, chair rail, and detailed molding work on the walls, we couldn't simply slap up the paint with a roller. We couldn't afford to hire professional painters either. We were lucky to have swung the mortgage. But I really needed the room to be painted Buffalo Grass Green before tomorrow. Nobody had beige walls anymore. Look at any magazine.

Since junior high, magazines have counseled me on every subject from acne to zinc. My mother had been fantastically useless in this regard. When home from work, my mother, Marjorie Darcy, had spent all her time clipping newspaper coupons for things like Scour-All and Whiffy Air Deodorizer. Later she'd gotten into crafting. I guess that ill-fated mummy outfit had sparked a creative fire in Marjorie. She had subsequently spent a lot of time turning empty Scour-All containers into plastic geese with crocheted wings and macramé hangers. Then, quite unexpectedly, a broken condom had resulted in a late pregnancy for my parents. Naturally, the new baby stole what little attention had previously been devoted to me. So I'd escaped to my magazines.

I think I realized even before puberty that I was a misfit in my family. I was a "misfit" because from a very tender age I realized that the world extended beyond the borders of our little town in central New York State. I recognized my worldliness in every conversation I had with my parents. For example, they could carry on an entire dinner conversation about the discount table at Schucker's Hardware. A whole dinner spent discussing dinged up plastic goods and miscellaneous screws. They either didn't know or didn't care that Al Schucker was the son of an exiled Nazi residing in Argentina. (Polly had told me so obviously it was true.) Why weren't we talking about *that*? How could they be so myopic? My parents treated me like I was from Mars and that was fine with me. Magazines filled the void left when they began devoting all their free time to the far more comprehensible, drooling infant that was my new sister, Kathryn.

Magazines are still an obsession with me. My favorites are the decorating magazines that I strew about my coffee tables and the celebrity gossip magazines that I read surreptitiously in the grocery store parking lot. I also dutifully read every fashion magazine I can get my hands on each month. I find many of the outfits unworkable for the real world. *My* real world, anyway. But fashion magazines saved me from complete exile during adolescence and I can't seem to kick the habit. A working knowledge of designer brands makes for good girl talk, even when your parents' (or husband's) pocketbook doesn't allow for purchases at stores that don't end with "Mart."

I managed to stay on the fringe of popularity with the junior high crowd in this way until I branched out into theatre and art during high school. Then I'd simply been weird. Of course back then, I'd pretended not to care, cloaked as I was with the power of creativity. I liked to think that I had become cutely eccentric. All the school outsiders found their way to the drama department and

I was their queen. Well, co-queen with Jon Pantor who was an actual queen who dropped out of school and moved to San Francisco. This phase had lasted until I met Jeff in college. I turned a corner in the English quad, bumped into Jeff and had been Scour-alling my "cutely eccentric" past ever since.

I looked around the room. Jeff had taken the day off from work to help finish painting the living room in time for my brunch. A lonely Christmas tree stood in the middle of the otherwise empty room (save a few drop cloths and the ladder).

"You left the invitation up on the computer, Janice. Sorry, I assumed you would fix the mistake before you mailed them out. I should have said something, I guess."

"Christ, Jeff. You know how important this party is to me. I want to make a good first impression. These are our new neighbors and I want them to like me."

Jeff paused in his work and turned on the ladder to face me. "No you don't. You want them to elect you Grand Pooh-bah of the Beach Park Better, Best and Bestest Club. Then you'll proceed to belittle them."

"What are you talking about?"

"Your usual M.O. All you used to talk about is how superior Beach Park was to our old neighborhood. We simply 'didn't belong' in our old neighborhood. We 'had' to move. Well, we've been here one month now and all I've been hearing about is how superior our house is compared to the others on this block. How there's a blue house with at least three weeds. How somebody has fake wooden shutters. How so-and-so has no eye for exterior tints. What the fuck does that even mean?"

"Jeff, you know I . . ."

"I know you *what*? I know you were dying to buy a house in this neighborhood, any house, and here you are already putting down our neighbors. For all your crying about never feeling like you belong, the truth is that you're just a snob who's incapable of relating to anybody."

"Where is this coming from?"

Jeff paused and visibly cooled off. "Sorry. Sometimes I'm afraid that I married my mother."

Ouch, I thought, mentally ticking off about a dozen smartass retorts. Instead I opted to look at the big picture. I needed the living room painted. "Look, Honey, I'm sorry I'm so stressed about this little party tomorrow. Hey, if they don't like me because of an invitation typo, then I'm better off knowing it right off the bat. Don't you think?"

Jeff smiled. "I think." To my great joy, he turned around and began painting again. I don't know what's worse: my manipulation or his passive-aggressiveness. We can't seem to break this pattern. At least the painting is getting done and that I *know* is a good thing.

I retreated into the kitchen where Marcy was doodling on the refrigerator with markers. I hoped Marcy hadn't heard Jeff and me arguing. We'd been arguing a lot since our move to South Tampa from Carrollwood, a neighborhood about ten miles to the north. It seemed like everything about Jeff was annoying me. Even his clothes. *Why is he wearing a stupid company golf shirt on his day off?*

"Marcy, Honey, you're supposed to draw on paper. Your tablet is on the kitchen table. Here, help Mommy clean off the fridge." *Thank God for washable markers.* I poured myself a second cup of coffee and pondered the last details for the party. The invitation glitch didn't bother me too much, now that I thought about it. Mr. Sarcastic and his perfect mother were the only ones who would ever notice. I dabbed at Marcy's artwork with a wet paper towel and Marcy retreated to the table.

I'd invited most of the women on my new block over for brunch tomorrow as a sort of Here-I-Am-Let's-All-Get-Acquainted party. Jeff called it my debutante ball but I was not amused. This was serious. I had never once hosted anything like this and I desperately wanted to make a good impression on my neighbors. I had been dreaming of moving to South Tampa ever since we'd moved to the Tampa area several years ago.

Tampa, like most cities of any size, has considerable sprawl. There are pockets of wealth here and there, certainly along many of the desirable waterfronts. South Tampa has its own special cachet. South of Kennedy Boulevard, and generally speaking, north of Gandy Boulevard (and anywhere by the water), South Tampa encompasses old neighborhoods, private schools, little boutiques, and non-chain restaurants (or restaurants that hide their "chain-ness" in a closet). Huge trees, narrow streets, and close access to downtown accent its charm. My friends in our old neighborhood had thought I was crazy to want to relocate. They view South Tampa as fraught with crime, inflation, and inconvenience. And there aren't any deed restrictions. What if somebody parked a clunker on the grass next door to you? *More like, wow, what if all of our mailboxes don't match. Tragedy!*

Jeff hadn't been convinced about moving at first either. He was a car salesman in Carrollwood so he had seen no reason for wanting to relocate other than what he considered my "social climbing" desires. Since parking his own ambition somewhere along Interstate 95 during the move down to Tampa, Jeff had become complacent. He used to talk about having a big house and expensive cars – about moving up the corporate ladder. I'd been the freer spirit early on in our marriage. ("Free spirit" was the nomenclature I had adopted when "cutely eccentric" didn't pan out.)

After a high school career built on one embarrassment after another, I'd finally accepted my niche with the artsy types in the fine arts program at college. I'd even revealed to these college friends my deepest secret at the time: my parents were school janitors. You know, those coverall wearing ghosts that lurk around school hallways and locker rooms making everything nice for society's self-absorbed youth. Clad with a sort of blue-collar snobbery and a flamboyant demeanor, I'd hung around the art department long enough to get a degree. Even at the time, however, the artist persona had felt like a warm blanket – something to be discarded when life heated up a bit.

Then I'd met Jeff, an MBA student with expensive clothes and an attraction for unconventional girls. Like me. Ones who had minds of their own. After years of feeling like an outcast, I was suddenly, rather inexplicably, "in." And with a boy who spoke my desired language of money, clothes, cars, and prestigious careers. A boy from Florida, not stodgy middle New York. Perhaps I injected whimsy into his life. He certainly injected security and possibility into mine. I'd dedicated myself to supporting his ambitions.

Now he used phrases like, "quality of life" and "me time." He actually liked it that he didn't have to wear a suit to work. Secretly, I hoped the old hungry MBA Jeff would pop back out now that the role models of South Tampa surrounded us.

I hadn't really sold Jeff on the moving-to-South-Tampa idea until a house on the fringe of Beach Park had become available for an almost affordable price. His mother lived in Beach Park so we would be closer to family. And wouldn't that be better for his mom whose second husband, John Dower, had passed away a few years ago? And wouldn't that be better for Marcy? Wasn't that why we'd moved to Tampa to begin with?

So we'd bought the house, a twenty-five year old two-story Colonial on a heavily treed block in the buffer zone between the newly constructed mini-mansions of Beach Park and the small, older rentals close to Kennedy, the commercial thoroughfare that forms the northern boundary of South Tampa. "Between the Ritz and the pits," Jeff had commented when we'd first looked at the house. So I had accused him of being snobbier than me. The house had needed only a little work — just some paint and the replacement of a few cracked windows. Jeff applied for the mortgage.

"Mommy?" Marcy mumbled from across the kitchen. I finished wiping the fridge.

"Mommy?" Marcy said again. "EXCUSE ME PLEASE!" she yelled from the table.

"Yes Honey, what is it?"

"What are snooty pants friends? Daddy told me to ask you."

"*Jeff!*"

2. Potential Interference

After dinner, Jeff put Marcy to bed and I played the closet game. I'd bought a new outfit for the brunch but at the last minute, older options beckoned. The first thing I tried on was what I affectionately referred to as my Slim Suit. It had been my fallback position for countless last minute dinners with Jeff's bosses and acquaintances (a.k.a., potential clients). Jeff wasn't just a car salesman. He sold pre-owned, certified, luxury cars. Just don't call him a used-car salesman. Even Mister Secure-With-Himself avoided that moniker. He was very happy with his work. So damn happy, that after initially taking the job as something to do while he looked for a real job in Tampa, he'd stayed. Made a career. *Hello everybody, this is my husband Jeff. He has an MBA but he prefers to hock automobiles to people with the jobs he ought to be pursuing.*

The navy blue of the Slim Suit sets off my eyes nicely and never fails to make me look ten pounds thinner. It also never fails to make me look like a Sunday school teacher. I started a reject pile. I didn't want to come off as too conservative.

The second and third outfits were similarly rejected: too worn and too tight. When did that happen? I checked the tag. Size 10. *Hmmm, must have shrunk. Maybe some slacks...*

Most of my closet's contents were piled on the bed when my old friend Margaret called.

"Janice, hi! Guess what? I'm actually going to be in your neighborhood tomorrow. I'm going to apply for a job at the Sears store. Wouldn't it be great if I got the job? I'd get to see you so much more. I already miss you in the neighborhood and it's only been like a month."

I had lived around the corner from Margaret Oaks for three years. We'd talked on the phone or in person almost daily. We'd seen each other in pajamas, with baby barf all over us, with dirty hair, whatever. It had been a comfortable, sisterly relationship. After I moved, I'd assumed that we'd keep up the phone chatter but there'd been some drifting in our friendship. Margaret might be a little jealous. After all, Margaret is divorced and has to work to support her two sons. Even if she gets the new job, she never could afford to live in South Tampa. I have it pretty easy by comparison.

"So, yeah, Margaret. It would be great to get together. What time is your interview?" I held my breath. *Afternoon, afternoon, afternoon*, I silently prayed.

"It's at ten. How about I swing by afterwards?"

It all flashed before my eyes: the Sears interview, Margaret's sloppy physique and her penchant for polyester, her terminally unkempt hair. Oh, and that voice. *Had Margaret always sounded like a chain smoker?*

"I'm sorry, Margaret. I have to take Marcy to the dentist tomorrow morning. Maybe I'll swing out to Carrollwood this Sunday. You're off then, right? But in the meantime, you call me and let me know how the interview went. Okay?" The lie slipped out without effort. *Scary*. I felt a faint pang of guilt.

"Of course I will. And bring your swimsuits so Marcy can go swimming with the boys this weekend. I've got the pool heated up to ninety degrees." Margaret did have a nice pool.

I replaced the phone and Jeff wandered into the room. He was wearing a tee shirt and a pair of boxer shorts. Jeff had an average build and nondescript features. His hair was straight and brown and tended to grow towards his nose on top and on the sides. It was actually pretty comical to watch him try and brush it away from his face without resorting to teenage-girly hair flips. He needed to wear it shorter. The smattering of freckles across his nose made him look boyish and outdoorsy, although his tendency towards freckling was exactly the reason why he shouldn't spend too much time out of doors in Florida. Not without being dipped in a vat of sunscreen first. Marcy had inherited his freckles but her hair was wavy, a lighter version of my own dark mop.

"Marcy's asleep. She wanted me to sing the national anthem but I had trouble remembering the lyrics. It's been awhile. Who called?"

"It was just Margaret."

"Is she coming tomorrow?"

That was a cheap shot. Jeff knew Margaret wasn't invited. "Were you able to get three coats of paint on today?" I shot back.

"Would I be showing my face if I hadn't? I'm going to read the paper now unless you have any further requests, Your Highness."

"Nope, you're dismissed, Footman." Despite the attempt at levity, the mood in the house was oppressive. Even I was getting tired of it. I resumed my closet search by trying on the new outfit again. It would have to do. Truthfully, nothing felt very comfortable.

3. Launch Day

The next morning dawned stormy and wet all across central Florida. NASA postponed a rocket launch. I should have followed their lead and cancelled my own launch plans for the day.

The first thing to go wrong happened in the living room. Jeff had removed the paint mess but had left the tree in the center of the room. I wasn't planning to entertain in the living room because it wasn't furnished yet. But I wanted to show off the room and therefore the tree needed to be in the corner by the window, gently oozing Christmas ambiance. The holiday was still a couple of weeks away but I had carefully wrapped a pile of empty boxes to display as gifts under the tree once it was in place.

I grasped the plastic under the tree and gently tugged the tree over to the corner. I was barefoot and my hair was still damp from the shower but sadly, I'd already put on my new outfit. So it was on the cheeks of my new slacks that I got raw, wet paint as I backed into the corner. Lesson learned – when the humidity level is up, don't pile several coats of paint on your walls in one day. The entire paint job had a sort of shimmer and sag to it.

"Mommy? Are the walls crying?" Marcy had walked into the room.

"No, Honey. Daddy just needs to start over in here. The paint didn't stick very well, did it?"

"Can we turn on the tree's lights?"

"Of course. I'll plug it in." With the tree lights on and the lamps off and the shutters closed, it looked almost pretty in the room with the sad walls.

"Mommy? You have a green bottom." Marcy commented as I dragged her into the kitchen for breakfast.

"That's Buffalo Grass Green, Sweetie. Thanks for noticing."

I left Marcy in the kitchen eating dry cereal and ran upstairs to change. Guests would be arriving in an hour so I had to hurry. Jeff had already left for work. It took him more than thirty minutes now to drive to his job. I decided to go for an artsy look. After all, I had an art degree. That would be a good conversation starter in a room full of guests that I didn't know at all. I just knew them by their houses.

I pulled my gently frizzing hair up into a neat ponytail and put on the hand-painted shirt I'd bought at a gallery in Orlando. I slipped on some khaki pants and hunted for my dark brown sandals. The television weatherman announced that the cold front blowing through the region would be gone by nighttime and that dryer air and cooler temperatures would follow. I went downstairs to check on Marcy.

"Sweetie, have you seen Mommy's sandals?" Forty-five minutes remained.

"Yes," Marcy replied without looking up from the sheet of stickers she'd found on the table. She was carefully placing the last of the stickers on the checkered dress I had chosen for her to wear that day. The stickers were of phony license plates with x-rated messages on them. Jeff must have brought them home from the dealership. All over her dress were stickers that said things like "FUK U" and "EATBEAV."

"Shit! You are going to have to change clothes Marcy. Those are Daddy's stickers and they aren't nice to wear." I pulled the dress off over Marcy's head.

"Why?"

"I'll explain later. Now where are my sandals?"

"I threw them outside up into a tree. And then two birdies flew away with them." Marcy's deadpan face revealed nothing.

Having raised the little imp, I understood this as Marcy-speak for "Sorry Mommy, I haven't seen your sandals today." I took Marcy and the dress back upstairs and put another dress on her. I raced back downstairs to warm the oven for my make-ahead egg and sausage casserole and the slice-and-bake Christmas cookies. Thirty-five minutes to go.

The phone rang. It was Margaret. She was crying.

Christ, why now? "What's the matter, Margaret?"

"Kelly wants to take the boys back to Illinois for Christmas. They'd be gone two weeks." Kelly was Margaret's ex-husband. They'd been divorced for two years.

"Doesn't he get them for holidays?" I stared at the clock. *Tick, tick, tick.*

"The holiday is one day, not fourteen." Pause, loud sniffing. "Whose side are you on, anyway?"

"Margaret, I'm so sorry to do this to you. You know I'm on your side. Do you want me to come over later this afternoon so we can discuss this properly? I might be able to leave Marcy with her charming grandmother. But I have to get off the phone right now because . . ."

"What time's the dentist?"

"What?"

"Marcy's dentist appointment."

"Oh, it's at ten – same time as your interview. Hey, shouldn't you be on your way? Don't let that jerk make you too upset to get the job you want."

"I won't." She sounded a little better. "I would love for you to come over this afternoon."

"Three o'clock. Be there or be square."

"Thanks Janice. I'll see you later." *Thirty minutes.*

The next half hour flew by. Promptly at ten, the doorbell rang. I smiled into the powder room mirror. No lipstick on my teeth. Too bad I hadn't had time to try out the new lipstick I'd picked up at the grocery store. The food was all artfully arranged on trays in the family room. I flipped on the Christmas music that had been playing nonstop on one of the radio stations since Thanksgiving and opened the front door to my guests.

The Blue House lady was the first to arrive. She had a little plant and a card. *How sweet!* The Fancy Mailbox lady arrived with the Twin Vans lady. I found out that they were best friends who sent their kids to the same preschool. Three Newspaper Lady told me that she'd seen Weed Lady who sent her regrets that she couldn't come after all. She had to take her car to some specialty shop that handled German imports. By the time the last of the guests arrived, nine women in all, I was impressed with the obviously high level of comfort and income they all seemed to enjoy. *Just look at those handbags!* I had assumed that the others on my block would be scraping by a little more, like Jeff and me. Their houses all looked so modest. *What a pleasant surprise.*

"Hello, I'm Janice Darcy. I'm so glad you could come. It's nice to meet you finally." Et cetera.

Of course, the realization that I had made some incorrect assumptions about my neighbors was followed closely by a crash in my self-confidence. I looked down at my hand-painted shirt and wondered how on Earth I'd ever thought that an impressionistic painting of two puppies peeking through tulips was even related to art. I was standing barefoot in front of this line-up of nine women with perfect coifs, perfect make-up, perfectly pressed cropped pants, and expensive shoes when Marcy descended the stairs in her original stickered frock with an extra sticker on her freckled nose for good measure. It read, "SUK 4ME."

Hello, I'm Janice Darcy and this is my little prodigy. And you guys were all high school cheerleaders, weren't you?

4. Mission Scrubbed

After an uncomfortable pause, I put on a bemused face and ripped the sticker off Marcy's nose. "Everybody, this is my daughter, Marcy. She's three and a half," I said with a wink, as though it explained everything.

"Marcy . . . Darcy?" Blue House asked.

"Oh no. She's Marcy Pintoff. Darcy is my maiden name."

"Oh, so you kept it?" Blue House asked again. I looked up to see eighteen eyebrows rise in surprise. Actually, only seventeen eyebrows went up. Twin Vans needed a pluck.

I smiled and changed the subject. I'd invested too much of myself in this brunch to lose it over some cultural differences. "I'm from New York State."

Seventeen eyebrows relaxed with such an understandable explanation.

"Let's go sit down, shall we?" I ushered them into the family room that suddenly looked very shabby. I bribed Marcy into the kitchen with a handful of cookies and invited everyone to grab some food while I poured coffee. Everyone wanted the coffee and virtually everyone drank it black. Then they quickly piped up about their favorite coffeehouse drinks that all seemed to have ten-word names: *I'll have a non-fat, half-caf, hold-the-whipped-cream, iced latte please.* Most of the food remained untouched despite the exclamations that I'd done such a nice job with the presentation.

The guests began talking amongst themselves, catching up on the latest.

Twin Vans: "Truman and Mary Blythe have Friday off for teacher conferences. Anyone want to meet at the playground? I'm sure I'll go crazy staying home with them all day."

Me: "Which playground?"

Everyone else: "Kate Jackson." *Of course.*

Fancy Mailbox to Plantation Shutters: "Are you going to the pool Saturday?"

Me to Plantation Shutters: "Don't you have a pool?"

Almost everybody: "We all go to the club on weekends." I didn't ask which one.

The next fifteen minutes were pretty much the same. "My book club is reading . . .." "The yard guy forgot to water . . .." "There's a sale at . . .." "My husband's firm . . .." "The Junior League is . . .." "At that last Buc's Game . . .." They sipped their coffees, dabbed with their napkins and seemed to forget all about me. Three of them even received cell phone calls. The cacophonous rings competed with each other for attention: Beethoven, Twinkle Twinkle, and whatever that one is that makes you say, "CHARGE!"

"So, we're finally going to redo the kitchen," Fancy Mailbox mentioned after putting away her phone. At last a topic on which I could expound.

"We've only been here a month and we've already tackled the living room. Well, started anyway. Just paint so far although we may need to reapply it."

"Oh, I haven't seen any trucks in your driveway. We all use this little man who does all the houses around here. He had a lot of trouble getting the shade right in our dining room. It's Ralph Lauren Hunting Coat Red. It took six coats. I'll get his number if you want."

"Oh, how nice of you." I remembered that Ralph Lauren paint was available at the same home improvement store where I'd purchased the Buffalo Grass Green. Might as well switch brands, I thought, if Ralph Lauren is what "we" are using these days. I was wondering whether I should admit that Jeff and I were painting the room ourselves when Marcy returned with a cookie-caked mouth and a blanched complexion.

"Mommy?" Marcy said before she spewed vomit all over Spanish Tile's trousers. I'm not sure whether I was mortified or relieved. Either way, the party was over.

5. Second Chance

That night, I scrubbed my face in the bathroom that I shared with Marcy. The master bath was too small to share with Jeff, who was hovering in the doorway watching me apply cold cream. Marcy was in bed.

"The doctor said it was a virus. She was a lot better this afternoon," I explained.

"Poor kid. Did she really get it right on that woman's lap?" Jeff made the snorty laugh noise that used to seem so endearing.

"It's not funny, Jeff." I was annoyed. I felt at once critical and defensive of my neighbors. I complained to Jeff as I washed my hands with soap out of Marcy's ducky dispenser. "You know, everyone else in this neighborhood has a pool. It's so that all the kids come to your house to swim and you can keep an eye on your own kids. You know how Marcy loves to swim. Maybe we should consider it."

"If everyone has a pool, then *nobody* is swimming together and everyone has a pool to take care of. Or maybe they all enjoy the same pool guy." Snorty laugh.

"I guess you take turns hosting or something. Anyway, everyone swims together at the club on the weekends."

"So we need to install a pool *and* join a club. Which club, might I ask?"

"I don't really know. Maybe you could make a couple of calls?" I looked hopefully at Jeff, ignoring his sarcasm.

"Sure, Janice. I'll dial up the mayor tomorrow and see where the in-crowd is swimming these days. Excuse me, I mean on weekends."

"Maybe you'd have more connections if you got a job downtown."

I was treading on familiar and dangerous territory. Jeff's voice rose to the occasion. "So once again my job is not good enough for you. Well, it bought you this house in a neighborhood full of people you were dying to impress. Or maybe you wanted them to impress you. I don't really know. I haven't figured out your disappointment of the day yet. Is it because nobody touched your pork-laden platters of food?"

I permitted full-fledged scorn to creep into my voice. "Maybe if you worked in an office downtown, we wouldn't have car-tag porn laying around the kitchen."

"Really, Janice. Look around. Even I could have guessed that half the women in this neighborhood are Jewish. And I'll bet at least half the women are vegans or something. Whoever that leaves is surely on a diet and you served bacon and ham."

"Sausage," I retorted. *Jewish? Vegetarian?* I swallowed part two of my retort. *Is that why there aren't many Christmas light displays around the block?* Thank God I'd at least scooped a few melon balls onto the brunch tray. I felt heartburn pressing in my chest. I changed the subject and my tone. "You know, we're going to have to put Marcy into preschool. Apparently everyone starts their kids out at age two in some school or another. Some kids even go five mornings a week. They were surprised I had Marcy home with me."

"Newsflash. Stay-at-home-moms generally stay at home — *with their kids.*"

"Well, yes, but now that we have this bigger house, I'll need more time to keep it up. Hey, at least I'm not asking for a housekeeper. It would be good for Marcy to interact with other kids her own age."

"Other kids her own age pick their noses and speak in two-word sentences. She'll think they are Neanderthals."

"Give me a break. These kids aren't like that. Never mind, you'll never get it." Marcy was another subject on which we could sharply disagree. I just wanted better for Marcy than I'd had myself. Wasn't that what parents were supposed to want?

"I do get it. You are measuring yourself against a group of women that you barely know and I'm not even sure you like. Worse, you're measuring our whole family against some standard that is impossible to define and therefore futile to strive for. You're making yourself unhappy, Janice. I warned you about this every time you made a pitch to move to South Tampa. Where's that free spirit I married?"

"Jeff, you don't understand and even worse, you don't care how I feel about this. I mean, God, these women were wearing the most exquisite shoes I have ever seen and I was barefoot. Can you imagine how I felt?"

"Comfortable?" Jeff smirked.

"Oh fuck you anyway." I stomped out of the bathroom and down the stairs as the phone rang. "And if that's Margaret, tell her Marcy got sick at the dentist and I'm sorry I didn't call her to cancel this afternoon."

"Marcy has a dentist?"

"Just do it." I sulked into the living room and turned on the Christmas lights. For the moment, I felt sadder than the droopy walls. Jeff had shown so much promise. Before relocating to Tampa, he'd worked his way up in a consulting firm in Syracuse. The constant business travel had bothered him and he'd been working for an ethically bankrupt partner but the pay had been good and the experience had been valuable. He and I had agreed after things fell apart with the old partner that after moving to Tampa to be near his mom, Jeff would seek work that kept him around home more often. Jeff left consulting behind with my blessing. I'd counted on him finding a suitable career replacement. I'd even signed him up for a seminar on self-actualization. He'd come home with a very disturbing interpretation about what it meant to be self-actualized. His explanation had sounded a little too much like laziness to me.

A few minutes later, Jeff walked into the living room holding a phone and covering the transmitter with his hand. "I got rid of Margaret, but you might want to take this call. It's from one of your *new* friends."

What a surprise! "Hello," I said as breezily as I could muster, turning away from Jeff.

"Hi Janice. Thanks so much for having all of us over this morning. I'm afraid we didn't get started out very well. We girls hardly ever get a chance to catch up with each other and then your little one got sick before we'd even properly got to meet you. I'm just so sorry about it all. Your house is really pretty, by the way. How is your little girl doing?"

My heart jumped with glee. All was not lost. Somebody cared. Was it Twin Vans or Plantation Shutters? Their voices sounded just alike. Sort of sweet and nasally. "She's doing fine . . ." I paused, hoping the voice on the other end of the line would identify itself.

"Well I'm so glad about that. Thurman gets those mysterious illnesses too. I just dose him up and send him to school. He's always better by lunchtime."

So it was Twin Vans. Or was her son named Truman? Maybe she'd said Thurman. It had to be Twin Vans. She'd seemed the nicest, really. She'd been all sunny and nice with a perky blonde ponytail and a giant sunflower on her handbag. I was about to offer another sick child anecdote when I was happily interrupted with music to my ears.

"Why don't you and your husband come by our holiday open house this Sunday afternoon."

I stammered a happy reply and quickly got off the phone. "WE"RE IN!" I shouted up the stairs to Jeff. "We're in, we're in, we're in," I sang as I skipped into the kitchen. Better call Margaret and find out how that job interview went. And cancel for Sunday. I'd have to tell Margaret that I'd forgotten about this "prior engagement." *Ugh, more lies.*

6. Cosmopolitans Socialite

On Sunday morning, I examined the damage that several days of extreme stress had done to my skin. In the past few days I'd shopped endlessly for just the right outfit and had also managed to paint the living room Ralph Lauren Mexican Feather Grass. Now, a large pimple had positioned itself as a second nose on my left cheek. Bags under my eyes were bordering on purple, a sure sign that allergies were at work as well. That would explain the sinus headache. I took some antihistamine and a pain reliever. Otherwise, I looked okay. The woman at the Clinique counter had sold me some special cover stick for the zit yesterday, along with a hundred dollars worth of skin care products and make-up. In an hour or two, I would be gorgeous.

The first thing to do was to remove all traces of mustache from my upper lip. I had purchased a hair removal kit at the drugstore. It was some foreign concoction that required no heat or other special equipment. I scraped some thick, purple substance onto the applicator and smoothed it across the skin below my nose. I pressed a cotton cloth onto the goo and yanked it away as quickly as I could. The sting brought tears to my eyes but when my vision cleared, I could see that the product had worked as advertised.

Not a single hair, dark or light, remained on that part of my face. My skin looked a little pink but that would fade. Time to shower.

My new dress was still hanging in store plastic from yesterday. It was a sleeveless black cocktail dress with a matching stole. I had always wanted a chance to go to a real holiday party in elegant clothes. Jeff's parties for the dealership always felt more like pep rallies. In my excitement, I could even ignore Jeff's protestations that he didn't want to go at all. Who cared if the Buc's game was going to be on network television? All the other husbands would be at the party.

At four, Jeff's mom arrived to watch Marcy. She was carrying a giant panda decked out like Santa Claus. It wasn't a gift. She just let Marcy play with it every year at Christmas. She would probably buy Marcy some sensible underpants as a Christmas gift. "It looks like there is more than one party going on today," she said as she swooped into the family room and scooped up Marcy. "What's that on your lip, Janice? You look like you've been drinking red Kool-Aid."

"Grandma – you brought the bear!" Marcy loved her grandmother. That fact kept me from alienating my mother-in-law too much. Right now I just felt a tremor of concern about the party situation. *It was at Twin Vans, wasn't it?*

I made Jeff wait by the front door while I checked my face in the powder room mirror. I applied some additional cover stick to the darkening maroon on my upper lip. Maybe I was having an allergic reaction to the hair removal goo. The red covered pretty well with the makeup. At precisely four fifteen we stepped out the front door in our finery and observed that there were in fact two distinct parties taking place in our neighborhood: at Twin Vans and Plantation Shutters. Cars were parked on every available stretch of street but guests were streaming up two different walkways.

"What's the matter?" Jeff had walked halfway across the grass while I was frozen on the front step.

"Nothing. Just double-checking that I didn't forget and put on a Christmas wreath pin or something. Wow, it's really bright out here. Maybe I should grab my sunglasses."

"Just come on, Janice. We're only going across the street."

And so I committed to my belief that it was Twin Van's invitation I had accepted over the phone. If I expressed doubt, Jeff would surely cancel the whole thing. We headed towards Twin Van's house. The matching Honda vans had been parked in the garage for the occasion. A couple of unfamiliar cars were parked in the driveway. Entry-level luxury cars, the type Jeff sold to people who would forego having all four tires if it meant that they could tell people that they owned a Mercedes, or whatever. As we walked up to the front door past the large picture window, we could see that the party was in full swing. A crowd of men and women stood with their backs to the window, chatting with each other over cocktail and wine glasses.

"Let's just walk in. I'm sure they aren't expecting us all to knock." I grabbed the door handle and pushed right in. Jeff followed a couple of steps behind me.

As my eyes adjusted to the light, I scanned the faces of those in the front room. I didn't recognize any of them and our hostess was not among them. I noticed straight away that everyone was wearing jeans and light sweaters. Mrs. Twin Vans had neglected to inform me about the dress code so I was massively overdressed. *No matter.* I immediately pulled an uncomfortable looking Jeff aside and told him to tell people that we had another party to attend right after this one. No time to change and all that. It was a trick I remembered from the fashion emergency section of one of my magazines.

"Hi, I'm Jan Darcy, well, Jan Darcy Pintoff. We just moved in across the street. The colonial over there." I gestured out the window for the confused looking gentleman whose hand I was shaking.

"Nice to meet you."

"I'm going to find a beer, *Jan*," Jeff muttered as he drifted off towards the back of the house.

"Ha, ha. I'll have the usual red wine dear. Thanks." I turned back towards the gentleman. I still had his hand. "Oh, there you are," I said as I returned his appendage to him. "I'm just a little flustered. We have a big party to go to over at the Wyndham right after this."

The man gave me a polite smile as he turned back to his conversation. The crowd in the living room was talking in a loud buzz. I pasted a smile on my face and pretended to be listening to whoever was nearest. I was actually straining to eavesdrop on a couple of smart looking women near the bookcase. I moved a few steps closer and couldn't believe my ears. They were being rudely critical of the Twin Vans' house.

"I would never have chosen that color for the couch. It doesn't match her room. She probably got it mail order," said the only woman besides me wearing a dress. Hers was a simple straight shift in a stylish color. *Anne Taylor maybe?*

"I'm sure I've seen one like it in my mailbox. I don't mind it but you can imagine that four thousand living rooms are sporting this exact same décor. Right down to the rustic birdcage and the Ralph Lauren designer colors. Why not spring for some original seating choices?" This woman had on jeans but they weren't the exact same model as those on the other women. They were a little more – something. I couldn't begin to guess the brand. I bought my jeans at the Gap.

"I heard they were going to have the office party at Armani's but she pretty much insisted that they hold it here instead. How she ever got so much clout, I'll never know. Maybe she's sleeping with George." Chuckle, chuckle.

I edged just a bit closer to more easily ingratiate myself. This was just too intriguing to pass up. I edged into the conversation. "Maybe *he's* sleeping with George," I offered. Chuckle. Snort. *Damn. Jeff's snorty laugh thing must be contagious.*

The two women cracked up. "I guess you've met George," one of them said, holding out her hand. "I'm Clara and this is Robbie. Who works at RCC, you or your husband?"

"No, no. We're neighbors just dropping off some fruitcakes for, you know, and then we're off to another party. At the Wyndham. I'm Jan. It's a pleasure to meet you."

"Well, Jan, you'll just have to have one of these." She handed me a drink off the shelf. A row of martini glasses stood brimming with pink liquid in front of the matched set of No-Home-Should-Be-Without classic books. "Robbie whipped them up in the kitchen." As Clara giggled, I realized that I was several drinks behind.

"So," I started, "do you guys have kids?" A safe enough topic.

"Three," Clara responded. "They're with their nanny right now. Hope is six, Marie is four and Trey is one and a half. Actually, he's Gordon Sillicott the third. We just call him Trey."

"Three. I get it. How about you?"

"Two little girls. Amanda and Louise. Do you have children?"

"Just one. Marcy is three and a half. Her name is really Marcella but everyone calls her Marcy." The lie jumped out of my mouth before I could stop it. Just a small fabrication, really. Nothing compared to the whoppers that popped out during the ensuing conversation. I was overcome with the desire to impress these women. I was pretty sure that my neighbors all dressed alike and went to the same salons and shoe stores in an attempt to cloak themselves in status. They were just hitting their marks on the societal obstacle course. They came off like a high school clique. But these two women, well they exuded some *real* class. Old Tampa, maybe? Obviously not wannabees.

Time flew by without me noticing or caring that Jeff hadn't returned after his hunt for a beer. It freed me up to recreate myself for these new friends. Never mind that in fact I had attended the wrong function. This was clearly Mr. Twin Vans' office party. Never mind that I hadn't departed for the fictional "other party" I'd been on my way to attend. I stood in the corner and drank Cosmopolitans with Clara and Robbie. Ms. Twin Vans popped her ponytail into the room occasionally but didn't notice me until fairly late in the party, largely because I had pretended to drop a napkin every time Twin Vans made an appearance.

"Hello, Janice," Twin Vans said when she finally caught up to me. "I see you know Clara and Robbie. Did you come with them?" Twin Vans was a vision in red and green holly printed what? A cat suit? Long johns? There were jingle bells on her shoes.

I bristled, but recovered quickly. "Oh, we go wayyy back," I slurred, while gesturing at Clara and Robbie. "Husbands in the same line of work, and all that. We were discussing the Gasparilla season." Gasparilla was a month long series of events that took place each late winter in Tampa. Sort of Tampa's answer to Mardi Gras. I was pretty sure that it was named after some legendary pirate. I was also pretty sure that besides the usual parades, art exhibits and fun runs, the festival involved a lot of fancy dress parties and things called "krewes."

"Your husbands sell used cars on the side?" Twin Vans asked Clara and Robbie. "I'll have to mention that to George." Twin Van's mono-eyebrow arched on the right side. A smirk worked its way across her lips. Luckily for me, Twin Vans was called away to attend to a finger food crisis.

"I guess she didn't like the fruit cake I brought." I wiped a bead of sweat off my lip as Clara and Robbie chuckled. Had I looked in the bookcase mirror, I would have seen the bright red stripe that had appeared above my lip as I wiped the make-up off my recent wax job. Clara and Robbie stared as though I had the plague. "Car salesman, as if," I added. I didn't notice Clara and Robbie staring at my lip and then over my shoulder at the man listening in on our conversation. "Jeff works at an investment firm. It's just a small branch here in Florida. I suppose someday we'll move back to the home office in New York. I love it there, don't you? I can't get enough of that Museum of Modern Art."

I paused and turned around. Jeff was holding a beer but judging from his bloodshot eyes, it wasn't his first. And he'd obviously been listening in on the conversation. "Excuse me," I murmured as I whisked Jeff out the front door, both of us tripping over imagined obstacles. But Jeff didn't stop with me on the front step. He stumbled on home without a glance back. I watched him safely navigate to our front door. And in a moment I regretted immediately, I returned to the party.

As I opened the front door, I was greeted by Mrs. Twin Vans herself.

"Janice, hello again. What's going on?" Twin Vans looked terribly confused beneath her ingrained haughtiness. "Is there something wrong with your face?"

"Oh, hello dear," I intoned loudly. "Lovely party. I believe this is your glass." I handed her the martini glass I'd been clutching. "By the way, everybody knows about you and George. Ta!" I waved over my shoulder and tottered back to my own dark house.

7. Singles or Doubles?

I felt the bed rumble as Jeff pulled on his socks with rough jerks and loud sighs clearly intended to rouse me. It was still dark outside.

"What time is it?" I asked as I decided against lifting my own head and looking at the clock. My forehead was suffering from Cosmopolitan abuse.

"Six thirty," Jeff answered. "I'm playing tennis with Derek at seven."

"Aren't you working today?"

"I told you yesterday that I was taking today off. I thought you'd be pleased about the tennis. Isn't it a gentleman's sport? Isn't that what all the big city executives play in their spare time when they aren't playing golf? Gee, I play golf too. I must make you so proud. Oh, but there's that little issue about me not choking myself with a tie every morning and not working so late in my downtown office that I never see you and Marcy, even when I am home from my weeks-long business trips."

"You know, when we met, you couldn't wait to get an office with a view. You wanted to be somebody." I propped myself up on one elbow.

"And you didn't. I mean you were a fierce individualist. Now you're trying your damnedest to be a lemming." Jeff shook his head. "I finally learn something from you, how to embrace life, and then I find out you've always hated yourself."

"I don't hate myself!"

"That's right, you just hate me." Jeff reached for his sneakers then turned directly towards me. His chin jutted out with tension "You should know by now that your disappointment in me isn't going to change anything. I've disappointed all the women in my life so far, no matter what I do. I'm sure you and mother cry together over my failures on a regular basis. But I refuse to disappoint Marcy and that means I need to be around."

"I understand your point . . ."

"No, you don't," Jeff interjected. "I mean I need to be around for her without being constantly attacked by her mother. Or her grandmother, for that matter." Jeff paused and lowered his voice. "I'm going to look for an apartment today. I think we need a break."

I rested my head back on the pillow. I squeezed my eyes to prevent tears from rolling down my temples onto the bed linens. *How had it come to this?* I loved Jeff. I loved the life I could imagine with Jeff. Why was I feeling so frustrated all the time? Why was he?

I ventured a counter plan. "Maybe we could get some counseling or something? Even Mr. and Mrs. Tidy Bowl went to a counselor when they had trouble."

"Are you too embarrassed by your parents to refer to them as mom and dad? I doubt anybody but you finds your nicknames cute or funny. What do you call *me* when I'm not around?"

My tears dried in their tracks. Criticism had a way of hardening me. "Maybe you're right, Jeff. Maybe a break is what we need," I said, wishing I'd sounded more sincere.

Jeff looked hard at me before getting off the bed. He picked up his racquet and headed for the bedroom door. He paused briefly. "This isn't over . . . We're not over, I mean. I love you Janice. We just need to get our groove back. I think a little space will help. I'll call you later, okay?"

Groove? Had my husband just used the word, "groove?" I stifled a laugh. Suddenly everything seemed downright hysterical.

8. New Year, New Resolution

I sat in Margaret's great room on New Year's Eve, waiting for the ball to drop. Piles of dishes were stacked on the kitchen island and more than a couple of champagne bottles littered the floor. Margaret was off checking on her sons who were back from an abbreviated trip with their father. I had a moment to contemplate my situation. First, I congratulated myself on the fact that I no longer lived in a house with a great room. Never mind that when I had, I'd made fun of houses like my new one with that dust-catching formal room in the front with no identifiable use other than showing off the Christmas tree to the neighbors. I looked around Margaret's living room for more things to besmirch, putting off contemplating my own situation a little longer.

"Have you heard from him?" Margaret asked as she came back into the room. We could talk now that Marcy was asleep. Marcy always slept like the dead. She'd insisted on staying up with us but had finally succumbed to sleep at around eleven, her hand stuck in a popcorn bowl and her head lolled back on a cowboy pillow.

"Not since a week ago. Christmas. Marcy spent the day with him and his mom. He got Marcy a remote control car and a pass to Busch Gardens." Jeff had moved into an apartment in Carrollwood. *A trial separation, maybe a divorce, who knew?*

"That sounds nice."

"Mags, she's three. She likes tea sets.:

"Come on, tell me she isn't going to love going to Busch Gardens. She'll probably divide all the animals up by genus or whatever. At least *your* ex still lives in town."

"Yeah, whatever. And he's not an 'ex' yet."

"What did your mother-in-law get Marcy? *My* ex-mother-in-law just loves to buy the boys hardback encyclopedias. She's never heard of the internet." Margaret was glowing under the track lights. Probably the champagne. But I was beginning to wish Margaret wouldn't act so chummy about my separation from Jeff.

"She gave Marcy pink clogs."

"Junior mule slides?"

This made me giggle so I forgave Margaret (for the moment) for being a little too glad to have me joining her in the single-mom club.

"So Kathryn called last week," I supplied during a lull in the conversation.

"How is your darling sister?"

"She goes by Kate these days. She's a big twenty something now."

"I can't believe she's twenty."

"I can't believe it either. Another Darcy daughter survives childhood and is sent into the world outfitted with hand-knit sweaters and framed needle points for the walls of her first apartment." I took another sip of champagne. "So of course Kathryn is royally screwed up and hasn't actually left the nest yet."

"Is she going to go to college?"

"Some day, I hope. She's looking for work, which she can't find in my hometown. Mom and Dad would never make her work but of course the price of that is too high. She's dying to move out of their house. I told her to move down here. There's a lot of jobs around here and then I can talk her into school."

Margaret looked surprised. "You invited her to live with you?"

"Sure. I could use a babysitter and as the older sister and only reasonable mother figure in the picture, I feel it's my duty to straighten her out and give her a proper send-off into the world."

"I always thought you weren't that close to Kathryn."

"Things change." I paused before emptying my glass. "Here's to change."

"Here, here," Margaret echoed, raising her glass. "Not to change the subject or anything but I must say, you don't seem very upset. About your separation, I mean. Do you hope things work out with Jeff? I can't tell." Margaret took a slow sip of champagne.

Immediately I felt like I needed to relieve myself in the bathroom. It happened every time I thought about Jeff. So naturally I tried to avoid such thoughts. "I'm not sure. I wish you could have known him before we moved to Tampa. He was so ambitious. I don't really know why he's become so . . ."

"Become so *what*? So good at doing what he likes that you can all live comfortably on one income? So infatuated with his family he wants to spend lots of time with you?"

I heard Margaret's sarcasm veer a little close to resentment. "Now you sound like him. I just mean that since he left, I'm beginning to wonder if he's the one who's held me back lately. I feel like everything is possible right now and I just want to enjoy the feeling for a while. I guess we'll see what happens."

"That's honest. This all must be pretty hard on Marcy though. I know my boys were really upset when their dad moved out. Heck, they still are."

"You know Marcy. She's different from most kids."

"So you are always saying. How are you settling into the new neighborhood, anyway? You must be making some new friends there."

"Well, sure, but it's a slow process you know. I'm discovering that there are a lot of things about South Tampa that I didn't know. But I'm a quick study. You know me; I'll fit in if it kills me. I'm so obviously meant to be there."

"Oh, *obviously*," Margaret mumbled as she sipped a little more champagne. "You know, it doesn't seem like it ought to be that hard."

"Well, nothing that's worth it ever comes easy. Does it?"

"Whatever, Janice. Just don't be a stranger around here."

I couldn't promise. The drive to Carrollwood already seemed a lot longer than it had before I'd moved south. Although I only lived a couple of blocks south of Kennedy Boulevard, that magic dividing line, my entire focus was now towards the south. I was beginning to understand why people conducted their entire lives SOK (south of Kennedy). Everything you might need could be found there. So what if the streets were narrow and had a tendency to flood? Drive an SUV. So what if you need to dress up a little nicer to go grocery shopping? At least you ran into all your friends at the store. So what if for the same money you could buy an entire estate on the outskirts of town? Then you lived on the outskirts of town. I wanted to be in.

"Say, can I ask you a personal question?" Margaret asked.

"Since when do you ask permission?" I sat up.

"What are you going to do about money?"

I slumped back down. "Good question. Jeff is going to support Marcy and help with the mortgage and stuff. At least for a while. But there's no way he can support me on top of that and I know he doesn't see it as his responsibility. Sometimes things can really come back to bite you on the ass. I made such a big deal about Marcy needing preschool that now Jeff says sure, and I can work while she's attending class. I'll have to figure out something."

"Sears is hiring part-time."

I closed my eyes so Margaret wouldn't see them roll. It was out of the question. "Sorry, Mags. I don't think my art degree qualifies me to hang clothes on plastic hangers. I'm not qualified for much of anything these days."

"Well, let me know if you change your mind. I have a little pull."

"Which department are you going to be working in at the new store, anyway?"

Margaret started laughing. "If I had a dollar for every time I've told you that I'm in financial management, I could retire. I swear you never listen to me. Do you like picturing me as a stock clerk? I have a master's degree in accounting, you know."

Actually, I didn't know. Interesting the things you can still learn about your friends after three years. "Sorry, Margaret. I'm feeling a little self-absorbed lately."

Margaret just laughed again. "Hey, I know somebody who is moving into your neck of the woods. Her husband is an attorney for some firm and she stays home with her two kids. Her name is Trudy. You two should get together. You can show her the ropes in South Tampa. She's been living in Lutz."

"Really? I just heard about somebody else who is moving to South Tampa from Lutz. I should start a consulting business."

And just like that, born from a joke, a business plan formed itself in my head. While Margaret cleared a few glasses, my mind reeled with plans. I'd have to start my research immediately. You probably couldn't buy your way into old Tampa society, but armed with the right clothes, cars, and connections, it shouldn't be hard to get welcomed into many of the sub-cliques. On this, I could become an expert.

"Margaret, you're a genius! I think I'm really going to do it. My Consulting Service. Well, that doesn't sound quite right but you get the idea."

"Yes and can I just go on record that this idea was not mine?"

"Come on, Margaret, be a sport. Give me your friend's number."

9. Fancy Schmancy

The next day, New Year's morning, I nursed a slight hangover, played Candy Land twelve times with Marcy, and compiled a list of potential consulting topics. I'd wanted to start my research immediately so before I'd even had a cup of coffee, I'd sneaked a look into my neighbors' driveways to see what newspapers they received. Lo and behold, everyone on this block took the Tampa Tribune. Of course, Ms. Three Papers got the St. Petersburg Times and the Wall Street Journal as well. Her husband was a banker or something. So at the top of my list, I placed "Reading Material." On a separate piece of paper, I made a note to myself to change to the Tribune. I liked the Times better but I could always buy copies at newsstands. It was all about appearances.

I would add subtopics to the Reading Material category later like, magazine subscriptions, and popular fiction. Right now I wanted to brainstorm about general categories. I added "Eating Out" and "Attire" to my list. Then the ideas really started popping: "Shopping," "Clubs," "Children," "Travel," "Neighborhoods," "Domestic Help," "Charitable Organizations," "Alcohol

Consumption," *scratch that*, "Suitable Drinks," and on and on. Some of the topics I pulled right out of the contents lists in my magazines.

Figuring that appearance would be high on anybody's list of priorities, I decided to start there. Kids would have to come next because every mom was interested in schools, parks, birthday party venues, and of course, children's attire. And children's issues would be the easiest to investigate because moms love to talk about their kids. Even to strangers at the mall. I made a note to take Marcy to the International Plaza to play on the playground there. It was the most upscale mall in Tampa and it was only a couple of miles away. It might even be open today. I'd have to check.

Marcy came into the kitchen and asked who was having a party.

"I don't know, Honey. What makes you ask?"

"Cars, cars, cars. I saw them out the window."

"Hmmm. Marcy, do you want to go for a walk with Mommy?"

"No." Marcy sat down at the table and picked up a colored marker.

"We could go get a pumpkin muffin at the bakery."

"And juice?"

"Of course, Sweetie. Go get your shoes and I'll help you put them on."

While Marcy looked for her sneakers, I primped quickly in the bathroom. I didn't know what I was going to do, exactly, but this seemed like an opportunity. I helped Marcy into her shoes and dragged her out the back door to head casually out to the front of the house via the driveway. Sure enough, there were cars parked up and down my stretch of the block. Twin Vans was hosting another something. *Didn't she ever get tired?*

I moseyed out to the front yard and tossed a ball to Marcy.

"I thought we were gonna go for a walk, Mommy," Marcy nagged.

"We will in a minute, Sweetie. Don't you want to play catch?"

"I play catch with Daddy." Marcy kicked at the ball. "We can kick."

"Whatever," I clenched. Another car was arriving. The family got out and headed up towards Twin Vans' house. I caught a break when Twin Vans herself strolled most of the way down her front walk to meet the arriving family.

"Hey there. Happy New Year!" I yelled and waved. I grabbed Marcy by the hand and dragged her across the street. "Are you having some family over?"

Twin Vans looked wary. "Well, yes. They're my husband's friends and family, actually." She was decked out in bright slacks and a red sweater with an appliqué of Baby New Year. There was a real diaper pin on it.

"Mind if we crash?" I asked.

Thunderstruck, to describe Twin Van's expression, would be putting it mildly.

"Oh, I'm just kidding. Say, I'm sorry about that Christmas party thing. My husband just saw a few people he knew going into your party and they invited us along, and well, we were supposed to have gone to a party at the Wyndham and I was a little upset with Jeff for crashing, but what can you do but go with the flow? Say, I really like your hair. Where do you go to get it styled? I'm looking for a new place now that we've moved."

"Thank you," Twin Vans answered. "I go to Fancy Clancy. It's not far. But there's kind of a long wait for new clients."

"Oh, I'm in no hurry."

"Actually, it's about four months or something. And it's kind of expensive."

I felt like I was being steered away from Twin Vans' hairdresser. That, of course, made me all the more determined. "Well, a good hairdresser is worth both the price and the wait. Maybe you can take me along next time you trim your hair and introduce me to your stylist."

"Well, uhm, sure I guess. Actually I just got it cut so it will be awhile."

"*Actually*, that's fine by me. Have a nice day. I'll call you." I left abruptly as the approaching family got close enough to be eavesdropping. I knew I'd made Twin Vans squirm and delighted at the prospect. Now, how to get in at Fancy Clancy? *Where was that place, anyway?* I'd find out and put it on my list of consultation topics. If I utterly failed to get an appointment anytime soon, I could at least find out the names of the hairdressers there. If nothing else, a person could get a cut somewhere else and drop the Fancy Clancy hairdressers' names. But that seemed like a last resort. *Where was that phonebook?*

Marcy pulled hard on my arm as I approached my front door. "MOMMY!!! MY MUFFIN!!!"

"Just a minute, Honey. I just remembered that I need to look up a phone number."

I found the yellow pages stashed on a bookshelf in my kitchen. Under "Hair Cutting and Styling," there was no mention of Fancy Clancy. *How exclusive*, I thought wryly.

Fancy Clancy would have to wait. But I wasn't giving up. I was going to befriend my neighbors and mine them for information. My conversation with Twin Vans was just a start. After all, my livelihood was at stake now.

10. Mall Rat

"Let's go get that pumpkin muffin and take it to the playground at the mall."

"Which mall?" Marcy asked.

"The animal mall. Won't that be great?"

"Yeah! I'll feed the dolphins some treats."

"Sure Honey." I helped Marcy into the car and drove over to International Plaza, stopping for a muffin along the way. The mall was open and the parking lot was crowded. We parked outside Nordstrom and walked through the store to the playground. Marcy stopped briefly to dance to the song being played by a tuxedoed pianist near the escalator. By the time we got to the playground, Marcy wasn't interested in the muffin anymore. She dashed off to climb up on a dolphin. Then she climbed down and pretended to feed it a snack. *Probably Goldfish crackers*, I thought.

Marcy bounced from the dolphins to the duck to the turtle to the turtle hatchlings and back to the dolphins. I settled onto the bench surrounding the play area. I sipped from my cup of coffee and scanned the crowd. The playground was busy with tykes of every size and shape. Most had on shoes, in direct violation of the playground rules printed affably on a sign shaped like a soda-pop cup. But I couldn't help noticing the quality of the shoes. And the colors. The girls all seemed to be wearing little jumpers bedecked with leaves or cute bugs and their little shoes seemed to coordinate perfectly – highlighting the bold accent colors of their clothing. Marcy was wearing her favorite pair of canvas sneakers purchased for a song at a discount shoe store. *And the dirt marks on her shoes nicely accent the stain on the front of her shirt. Ugh.*

The same sign that prohibited shoes also prohibited kids over forty-two inches tall from playing on the playground at all. I observed the assortment of lunkers hovering near the turtle eggs. The boys were at least eight years old and fixing to play a game of tag. Most likely, their mothers had dropped them off to play while they shopped. Sure they were nice looking boys. I was sure their trousers were nothing but the finest. But I saw the boys as a menace to the safety and well-being of my little girl, now posed as a singing cowboy on the back of a turtle. I made a mental note to keep an eye on the boys vis-à-vis Marcy.

I took another sip and looked around at the other grown ups. I pegged several as babysitters or nannies. They were dressed casually and wore a uniformly bored expression. One particular group of moms caught my eye, however. They were huddled up near a virtual parking lot of strollers. They were having an animated conversation and appeared to know each other well. All of them had perfectly adorable toddlers and I surmised that the group was having a play date at the mall.

Again, the first thing I noticed was the clothing. While I was dressed fairly nicely in name-brand jeans and expensive sneakers, these women were a vision in lime green capri pants, pink plaid, and a sort of loud patchwork pattern. One even had on riding pants. Their perfect hair, their matching accessories and their expensive shoes all spoke of something that I couldn't quite pin down. Mere affluence didn't explain it. There was a concomitant confidence. An easy style. They looked a lot like my neighbors, only less premeditated. I figured that these were legitimate trendsetters. After all, someone had to decide which styles and brands my neighbors would try to copy. I wanted to know more about them.

After making a quick check on Marcy (the thundering boy-herd was nowhere near her), I looked for a way to get close enough to eavesdrop on the women. I wouldn't have to get too close. They were speaking very loudly in order to hear each other. Occasionally their heads rocked back in laughter. I noticed the group's proximity to a waste receptacle placed just outside the play area. I picked up my coffee and slugged down the whole of it with my back to the group. Then, making an overt effort to seem to be looking for a waste can, I gathered my purse (a black leather nothing) and casually strolled over to deposit my empty cup in the can.

Nobody so much as glanced at me as I made my way over to the trashcan. *Good.* The door on the can was covered with candy goo and God knows what. I didn't want to touch it. I pushed gently at the door with the cup but the cup wasn't strong enough for the stiff hinge. Glancing about first, I used the bottom of my purse to shove open the door to deposit the coffee cup. My purse stuck on the goo and the long purse strap dangled just enough to get caught in the door as it banged shut. *Shit.* Just then, a blood-curdling scream emanated from behind the furthest dolphin. It was Marcy. I couldn't see her but judging from the collection of punks on top of the dolphin where Marcy had been sitting, I gathered that Marcy had been knocked down.

I pulled hard on my purse strap and it escaped the clutches of the trashcan but not without pulling the can over with a loud clang. Dirty napkins stuck to my purse strap. The can continued clanging as it rolled back and forth on the tile floor. Marcy continued to scream and under the lash-curled gaze of those brightly clad women, I straightened up, plucked off the napkins, and ran as fast as I could to my crying daughter.

"Marcy, are you okay Honey? Are you hurt?"

I knelt down beside Marcy on the far side of the dolphin, shielded from prying eyes. The boys looked apologetic and offered an explanation. I just hissed at them to get out of the play area before I called a security guard.

"I'm okay, Mama," a now softly weeping Marcy assured me. "I fell down."

"Does anything hurt?" I couldn't see any signs of damage.

"No. But they stepped on the dolphin treats."

A wave of relief swept over me. Marcy was fine. I picked her up and gave her a hug.

"Yucky. What's on your purse?"

"Try not to touch it Honey. Mommy got it kind of dirty. I'll wash it when we get home. How about we get going?"

"Uh huh," Marcy agreed.

I turned around and glanced back towards the group of women. They weren't paying attention to Marcy and me at all. They were talking to a man and a woman that I recognized. The woman was wearing similar clothes to the rest: a plaid skirt and a tasteful top. In fact, the plaid of her skirt matched the plaid on another woman's pants. *Must be the latest*, I thought. *Or maybe I've been reading the wrong magazines.* The woman turned out to be Weed Lady — my neighbor who hadn't been able to make it to the brunch. I would recognize that pert blonde bob anywhere. The man was my husband Jeff. He was wearing a stupid company golf shirt, and a smile.

11. Betrayal

I picked up Marcy and scurried away from the play area. I was pretty sure Jeff hadn't seen us and more importantly, Marcy hadn't seen Jeff. I exited the mall through a side door and had to walk quite a long way around the mall to get back to where I'd parked. I fished out my phone and dialed up Margaret.

"Hi, thanks again for last night, yadda, yadda. But that's not why I'm calling. I'm totally freaked out here!"

"Where are you?" Margaret asked.

"International Plaza," I responded as I lowered Marcy to the ground and held my hand for the walk to the car. "I just saw J...E...F...F and he was with the Weed Lady!"

"Who's the weed lady?" Margaret asked.

"J says juh," commented Marcy.

"That's right, Honey," I noted to Marcy. "Weed Lady is one of my neighbors. She's the only one who conveniently couldn't make it to my brunch," I said to Margaret.

"What brunch?" Margaret inquired.

"Not important – just a neighborhood thing I had before Christmas. Anyway, I'm shaking here. Do you think it's even possible that J...E...F...F is dating already? Dating *her*? My god, he gave me so much crap about trying to fit in and look at this! She's not even very beautiful. Cute maybe." I bit my lip to keep from crying. "I can't believe this!"

"E says eh," said Marcy.

"Great, Sweetie." I fanned my face with my free hand. "Margaret? Are you there? Say something."

"I'm thinking. You said Weed Lady . . . what's her real name, anyway?"

"I have no clue."

"No matter. You said she stayed away from some brunch you threw for the neighbors."

"Right."

"Well, doesn't that make you wonder if something was going on before you even split up?"

I couldn't respond. I'd been so distraught about the thought that Jeff was dating that a previously established affair hadn't even yet posed itself as a possibility.

"F says fuh."

"Right, Honey."

"JEFF!!! You spelled Dada's name, Mommy. What is dating?"

"Does it *really* bother you? Last night you sounded like you were ready to move on, start a business," Margaret inquired.

"I'll call you later, Margaret." I turned off the phone and unlocked the car door. "Get in Sweetie. I'll explain later. Good job spelling." *Why can't you be interested in dolls and bugs like normal three year olds?* I actually appreciated Marcy's intelligence and her unusual view of the world, I just hated that I couldn't spell out commentary in front of her anymore. Time to get her into preschool.

I evaluated my immediate feelings as I drove home. I was hurt and jealous that Jeff had somebody else on his arm – that he obviously didn't need me. But I was even more alarmed to discover that my reaction just made me feel desperate and needy. Dependent. Awful. Thank God I had plans of my own!

12. Marjorie, Kate and Ted

Suddenly the afternoon appeared interminable. Completely unsettled by recent turns of event, I had a hard time focusing on Marcy who was making her usual demands about lunch (no crusts, no bread with nuts in it), television (no shows with real people), and assistance requirements in the bathroom ("Mommy! The poop is too big. I need help wiping!"). I was mid-wipe when the doorbell rang.

"Just a minute," I shouted. *Is it Jeff?* Suddenly I needed to go to the bathroom myself.

I opened the door to my sister, Kate, née Kathryn.

"You're here?" I asked. Kate stood before me on the front step. Kate was lovely, or had been before she'd pierced her eyebrow, tattooed her ankle and adopted a rather individual style of dress. I could just make out the barbed-wire design below Kate's hemline. Kate's skirt was a homemade ensemble with several layers of what appeared to be some little boy's sleeping bag liner — the kind with brown cowboys on a red background. Her dark hair was swept up in a ponytail. She didn't wear any make-up so it was easy to see our parents' genetic marks on her: Dad's pointy nose, Mom's (and my) blue eyes, and every Darcy's square jaw line. She was shorter than me but annoyingly thinner.

"Surprise! I said I would take you up on your offer."

"How did you get here?" I looked out to the curb for a taxicab and was startled to see my mother's beat up Toyota. "Mom gave you the Camry?"

"Mom drove me down."

I looked again. *Yep, sure enough.* There was Marjorie Darcy. She'd been bent over something in the back seat. Now she was climbing out of the car. Now she was walking up the driveway. Now she was close enough to say hello. And still I was pinching myself to wake up from this surreal dream. I hadn't seen my mom in a long time. I had mostly relied on updates from Kathryn when she'd occasionally phoned. I had been hiding for a long time behind the pile of resentments that had built up during my adolescence. That was easy long distance. Now here was Marjorie in the flesh.

"Mom?"

"Surprise, Sweetie. Where's my little girlie?"

It took me a second to realize that Marjorie was referring to Marcy, not me. *Nice to see you, too. Thanks for the warm hug.*

"Bathroom. So how long are you staying, Mom?"

Marjorie ignored the question and breezed past Kate and me who were still in the doorway.

I lit into Kate. "What's going on? Mom smelled like perfume. She doesn't wear perfume. Since when does she go farther than the grocery store without Dad? Kate, did you make her drive you down here? You really should have flown. How is she going to get back?"

Kate smiled and rolled her eyes. "Mum's having a bit of a mid-life crisis. She quit her job. Can I come in or what? I like your new digs, by the way." *Was that a fake British accent?*

I followed behind my sister. We found Marjorie in the kitchen with Marcy. She was snooping through the pantry. Marjorie looked older and slightly thicker but less unkempt than I remembered her. She was wearing a conservative navy jacket but underneath, I swear I detected tie-die.

"So Mom, have you become a Dead Head? You know that they aren't touring anymore."

Marjorie regarded me sweetly. "I understand your confusion, dear. You always make a funny little joke when you're uncomfortable. Ted said you probably would."

"Who's Ted?" I looked at Kate.

"Her guru."

"I'm just taking a little life-break to figure a few things out. I guess you should know that I have separated from your father."

I glared at Kate.

"Told ya."

I turned back to my mom. "Mommy, *Kate* was your mid-life crisis. You don't get two. Besides, unless you are going to live past a hundred and twenty, you are way past mid-life."

"Who said anything about a crisis or mid-life?"

Marjorie's calm demeanor began to infuriate me. *Who is this Ted? Is he having an affair with my mother?*

"She thinks she might be gay," Kate interjected. "Is the guest room upstairs? I need to get the road dust off of me."

"Marcy, will you take Aunt Kate up to the guest room? Now?"

Marcy grabbed Kate's hand and led her through the swinging door of the dining room. I looked at my mom who had turned back to the pantry and was now pulling out a box of pasta. "Mom?"

"You know, nothing satisfies like a bowl full of starch. Ted says I should stick to eating raw food but I just can't seem to give up spaghetti. I'll make some for all of us. Where are your pots?"

"What's going on, Mom? You can't just run away from Dad and decide you're gay and move in with me."

"Which of those things bothers you the most? Oh, and where do you keep your oregano?"

"Mom? Are you listening to me?"

Marjorie faced me, clutching the noodles to her chest. "Of course I am, Sweetie. That's why I'm here. To listen to you. Ted thinks it's time we mended our relationship and to do that, I need to be close to you. If you ask me, the timing is perfect. What with you approaching mid-life and having a crisis with Jeff and all that. The oregano is where?"

I pointed to a cupboard. I was remembering when I was little, maybe ten, and my mother had taught me how to test spaghetti for doneness. You pulled out a noodle and threw it at the wall. If it stuck, it was done. Of course, by modern standards it was way overcooked at that point but I felt myself looking around for a smooth wall in my kitchen for my mother. Then I backed out of the room and let my mom make her comfort food. *What kind of guru is named Ted?*

13. Priorities

That night, I took a bath instead of a shower — a long, steamy bath with bubbles (*potential urinary tract infection be damned*) and a bottle of wine. I had to empty the bath once when the glass candleholder exploded but I remained undaunted. I cranked up the monitor for Marcy's room in case my little darling woke up needing me and then I did the closest thing to meditation that I could think of: I listened to a Bing Crosby Christmas album (cassette tape, actually) from start to finish. Never mind that Christmas was over. I remembered to sing along with every skip and crackle, just as I had as a kid when my parents had played the same album on their hi-fi.

And now my mom was here. And my sister. How could their timing be worse? I had a business to get off the ground. Mom professed to want to patch up our relationship but I felt pessimistic about that mission. The few times I had tried to smooth things over with my mom, she had become embarrassingly apologetic and weepy. Now that it was my mom's idea, she was all business-like. The new, gay, even-tempered, guru-channeling personification of my mother was going to take some getting used to. Of course it could all be a front. It would be just like my mother to one-up me in the neediness department. *Oh, you and Jeff split up? Well, your father and I have separated too and I think I might be in love with my water aerobics teacher. I'm just so confused.* Marjorie loved to be needy. I despised that about her.

And then there was Kate. I smiled. At least my sister had spirit. I planned to give Kate the advice she'd never received as a young woman. Neither of our parents had ever attended college and so college had been a sort of optional, go-if-you-can-pay-for-it affair for me. I'd really had to find my own way. Undoubtedly my parents had offered to pay Kate's way to college (another resentment topic as yet unexplored) but Kate was holding out. I felt duty-bound to steer Kate in the right direction. You couldn't become a successful businesswoman or a Senator's wife or even a teacher at a private high school with all those piercings and that strange wardrobe. You needed to be college educated and polished. *Poor, sweet, misguided Kate.*

Finally, I considered the whole Jeff issue. Was he having an affair with Weed Lady? Did he want a divorce? Would he fight for primary custody of Marcy? Or was he having a midlife crisis of his own? Maybe he would snap out of it. Did I want him to snap out of it? Fear and anger stewed inside me.

I emptied the tub and slipped on pajamas. I sat down on my bed with a notepad. *Time for a priority list.*

1. Find Marcy a preschool so I can focus on other priorities
2. Get mom to move back to New York ASAP
3. Find a job for Kate
4. Get a new wardrobe
5. Print up business cards (*Hmmm, what to name the company?*)
6. Organize consulting biz and schedule first meeting

7.   Research something to say at first meeting

8.   Find out something re: Weed Lady

I let my mind wander towards all sorts of sordid and evil number nines but I kept the list at eight. Best not to put into writing how I was feeling about Jeff right now. Best to heed Margaret's advice and focus on my own needs. Mine, and Marcy's of course. Marcy was the brightest light in my life and I wanted her to be happy.

I flipped the page and began listing the preschools I'd heard about in the last few weeks: five St. Whatevers, four you-name-it United Presbyterians (or Methodists), three Play Somethings (Nook, Time, and Place), two Jewish schools, and a partridge in a pear tree. *Okay, wine is going to my head. Time to go to bed.* I dropped my list and my pen, leaned back and clawed my way into dreamland.

By eleven o'clock the next morning, I had found a preschool for Marcy. The Jewish Family Center had an opening in their three-year-old class that met five days a week until noon, or two o'clock if your child stayed for lunch. *Perfect.* Jeff's mom, Ol' Mule Slides, would have a cow about Marcy being in a Jewish school and that made the choice all the more appealing. Classes were resuming the next morning after winter break so all I needed to do was drop a check by the office and get a couple of medical forms filled out by Marcy's doctor. *Piece of cake.*

The next task of the day was a little more difficult. I needed to inform Marcy that her days of freedom were over and from now on she was going to have to conform to society's expectations of her. Before I got around to that, however, I needed to find my conspicuously absent houseguests. *You'd think they could leave a note.* The car was still out in front so they must have walked somewhere. Maybe to the mall? Mother and daughter arrived before I had more time to ponder their whereabouts.

"Hey Kate," I smiled, "and Mom. Kate, I was thinking about helping you with your resume today. Maybe we could get it ready to print out and then go get some expensive paper and envelopes. I saved the job listings in today's paper for you."

"Yeah, thanks, sis. I'm really not in a hurry though. Is it far to the beach?"

"Uhm, not too bad. Maybe half an hour."

"Cool. I've already got my suit on. Can I take the car Mom?"

"Of course, dear." Marjorie was unloading a small bag of pastries, a clue to where they'd been.

"I hope those pastries are raw, Mom, or I'll have to report you to Ted."

"I just got some goodies for Marcy. They're not for me and you don't need them, I'm sure. Where is the little girlie?"

"In her room," I squeaked through clenched teeth. *So now Mom thought I was fat.*

"By the way, I spoke to Margaret while you were on the phone this morning. I saw her number in the kitchen so I called her on your cell phone. She's dropping by here on her lunch break. I'm glad you two are still close. Margaret is such a good woman."

Good woman? "How would you know? You've never met her before."

"But you have talked about her so much over the past few years, I feel like I know her already. I'm happy to finally meet her. We women have to stick together you know. Maybe I'll make a salad. Does Margaret like avocados? Oh, who doesn't like avocados? Okay, now where is Marcy?"

"Her room, Mother. Since when did you become such a women's libber?"

"Feminist, dear. No need to treat me like I'm quaint." Marjorie left the kitchen.

God, my mother needs to go back home. Her home.

At lunch, Marjorie plied Margaret with food and the two of them began cozying up over a discussion of my future.

Margaret: "I think she should get a job at the mall. It's close. Something part-time, kind of flexible."

Marjorie: "Maybe she should open a breakfast slash lunch spot. Something cute and trendy. Maybe a raw food place."

Margaret: "So you've tried her cooking?"

Both: "Ah, hah hah."

Marjorie: "Don't you think she'll patch things up with Jeff? I really hope she patches things up with Jeff. It's hard for me to see Janice as a single mom."

Margaret: "I do. He's a pretty great guy."

Marjorie: "Janice's father and I have always thought so."

And on and on. When Margaret offered to hook Marjorie up with a woman that she'd met at her son's school, I left the room.

The next morning, I got up early, made Marcy some pancakes with smiley faces on them and picked out some fun play clothes for Marcy to wear on her first day of school. When Marcy came downstairs, bleary eyed and innocent, I nearly cried. *Was I doing the right thing sending Marcy to school?* But I fought the impulse to scrap the plan by remembering the big picture.

"Good morning, Honey. Did you sleep good?"

"Hi mommy. I slept well. Is it morning?"

"Yes, Honey. You can get up now. It just looks dark outside because of some clouds. Do you want some juice?"

"In a box. Apple." Marcy dragged herself out to the playroom, snapped on the television and seated herself on the brown leather couch.

"Why don't you come have your juice in the kitchen, Marcy. I made you a surprise – panny cakes."

"Is it Christmas again?"

I grimaced, remembering yesterday's kitchen yak about my culinary deficiency. Maybe I should try to cook a little more often. "No Honey, but it is a special day. Do you remember how we talked about you going to school someday?"

"I get to go to school?" Marcy interrupted. "Yay, yay, yay. I get to go to school, I get to go to school." Marcy ran around in circles and I wondered if I would ever be able to figure out my daughter. *Probably not.*

"Let's go now, Mommy." Marcy ran over to the television and turned it off. "I don't like TV anyway." Marcy ran over to the back door and my heart ached to see my little baby standing there in tulip pajamas and curly bed-head hair, so ready and willing to embark on her umpteen-year journey through the halls of education.

"We'll go when the big hand is on the ten and the little hand is almost on the nine. That gives us plenty of time to have a little breakfast and at least put on some shoes. I'll be picking you up at lunchtime."

"Oh, yeah. Okay, Mommy. And remember, don't comb my ears when you do the pony tail."

"I promise."

"And when I get home, can I watch TV with Nana?"

"Of course."

14. Intervention

I should have been suspicious when my sister offered to pick Marcy up from school. In the days since her arrival, Kate had spent all of her time dodging my inquiries about job hunting and basking in the weak winter sun at the beach. She'd also added a tattoo to her shoulder. It depicted some sort of sexy fairy butterfly from the rear. When Kate had asked for directions to Marcy's school that morning, I had foolishly believed that vacation time was over and Kate was stepping up to the plate. *Nope.*

"So honey, I hope you don't have any lunch plans today," my mom said in a girlish voice.

"Why, are you going to dig up some roots for me to eat? I think the azaleas are ripe." I was growing increasingly annoyed with my mother. All she did was watch Home and Garden television. When the TV was off, she practiced yoga or rearranged my furniture and accessories according to the principles of feng shui, her latest passion. When that obsession wore off, she would probably launch into polymer clay jewelry. I had found a book about that in the family room one day.

"I have a surprise for you. Margaret is coming by for lunch today."

"And?" There just had to be more to it.

"And she is bringing someone with her."

I gave Marjorie my most insincere smile. "And you aren't going to tell me who it is, are you?"

"Nope." Marjorie gave me back her most secretive smile.

I was left deciding whether Margaret was going to introduce us to her new boyfriend or a new girlfriend for my mom. *Please let it be a boyfriend for Margaret.* I couldn't accept the idea that my mom had left my dad. I really couldn't believe that my mother was gay. I hadn't had time to call my father although I thoroughly intended to do just that. Maybe he would come down to Florida and straighten my mother out. They would reconcile and head back north. I could put my furniture back and start my business. Kate could get a job and go to school. Marcy could be Marcy. I picked up the phone and dialed my parents' number.

My father wasn't home. I didn't leave a message because I hadn't thought through what it was I wanted to say. Later I would try again. He was probably at work.

When lunchtime arrived, Margaret pulled into the driveway at precisely twelve o'clock. Marjorie was peeking out the shutters. "They're here!" she squealed.

They turned out to be Margaret and Jeff.

"*Mom!*" My emotions included anger, fear, excitement, and concern over my clothes and lack of makeup. The mix created instant heartburn.

"Margaret and I just thought the two of you needed to sit down together and talk over some issues and Jeff agreed. Margaret and I will just keep you two on track. Like an intervention."

"You have got parenting all backwards, Mother," I steamed. "You were supposed to solve my problems when I was a kid. I don't need you to do it now."

Marjorie remained serene. "I'm not trying to solve your problems. I'm just helping you solve them yourself. Oh, here they are." Marjorie opened the door and the guests came in. Thoughtfully, they'd brought take-out food to the intervention. *Just what did one serve at this kind of event?*

Noodle bowls. With vegetables.

I looked around in disbelief as the three others spread the food around my dining room table. *Was that a tape recorder near my mother? How dare she meddle in my life? What happened between Jeff and me was my own business.* I took the only reasonable independent woman's course of action. I fled to my room.

If the intervention went forward, it went forward without me. I didn't ask my mother about it. When Kate brought Marcy home later, I left with Marcy to go to the park. My mom was in the kitchen making homemade modeling clay.

Jeff called that night to apologize. He hadn't known that it was a surprise for me. *Yes, yes, fine, fine. Let's talk later.*

I didn't know what to do. If I criticized my mother for springing Jeff on me, my mother would get all hurt and blubbery about only trying to help. If I ignored it, my mother might try it again, or worse. She might try to unleash Ted the Guru on me. Best to talk to Kate. Kate seemed to be in a better position to talk sense into Marjorie than me. As for Jeff, I fully intended to speak to him, but not now. Later. Someday. I decided to focus on my consulting business plans. It was the only thing I felt I could control.

15. Playground Chatter

With Marcy in school, it would be easier for me to conduct my research at the mall, although my stomach flip-flopped at the memory of seeing Jeff there with Weed Lady. But what were the chances of that happening again? I went there one morning after Marcy had been in school for a week with no signs of imminent breakdown. There was the minor issue of hanging out at a play area *sans* child. No matter. I just made my eyes follow an imaginary child around while I trained my ears on the playgroup huddle. It was no strain to listen in on their conversation. They were pretty oblivious to the rest of the world.

Today, as it was almost cold outside, the group was bundled up for winter. Most of them had on rah-rah college gear of some variety, even if it was as subtle as a belt. I noted with interest that all the team stuff was for college teams, not the Tampa Bay Buccaneers, although these women all probably held season tickets. I made a mental note to purchase a University of Florida or Florida State sweater or bag. Or maybe Georgia. Something southern, anyway.

They seemed to be discussing summer camp for their older girls. Apparently, South Tampa girls of a certain young age all got shipped off to North Carolina somewhere for a few weeks. I was slightly aghast until I realized that the families also seemed to own houses or timeshares up in the same area. So maybe the girls weren't completely abandoned by the family all summer. Also, it appeared that all the women had at one time themselves been dutifully packed off to North Carolina. *So it is something that is just done, huh?* I would check it out, of course, but I was thankful that Marcy was only a three year old. I would have plenty of time to adjust to the idea of sending my child a thousand miles away to make crafts with acorns, or whatever it was they did at camp.

I listened in for a while and laughed occasionally at my imaginary child. The next topic of playgroup discussion was more pertinent to me. The subject was school. Elementary school. As in pre-kindergarten for four year olds. *How many kids do these people have?* Apparently large families were back in vogue. For the families with older kids already attending elementary school, admission was a done deal for the younger sibs. Unless, of course, they were boy children with summer birthdays or total dolts. Then you had to hold them back a year to ferment a little longer. That explains the "transitional" class for five year olds at Marcy's new school. I had thought those kids had somehow flunked preschool. *Come on, how do you flunk finger-painting?*

I listened attentively. If you lived in a good public elementary school district, it was acceptable to send your child there. All these women knew other women who sent their kids to public school. If your child was ridiculously bright or, you know, disabled, public school was even an advantage in some cases. But really, the way these gals talked, the public school moms came off as funky alternative lifestyle acquaintances. Not integral members of their squad. *Normal* kids went to private school.

"I heard that Paige Tillgood is going to President's Elementary. When I was teaching there, before I got married of course, it was a pretty good school. There were a lot of really nice parents."

"Hmmm. Right. Still."

"Oh, I know, I just can't bring myself to send John Patrick there. But you know Shauna, she thinks Paige has something to gain from a public school experience."

"Yeah, I love Shauna. She comes to my bible study group. But she's always been a little out there. I heard she joined a grocery co-op."

"No way!"

Scratch public school.

The discussion moved on to private schools. Apparently, although it was only January, all the applications had been submitted and the kids were all scheduled for a series of school interviews. Decisions on acceptance could be expected around March. *Christ, it's worse than college.* I felt my heart knock a little louder in my chest. I was behind the game already and I'd just found out that it was being played. Time to hit up Jeff for next year's tuition and to hit up his mother to call in a favor or two to get Marcy on a list somewhere. *Nope, nope. Reverse that.* Discuss the social benefits of private school with Mule Slides and let *her* convince Jeff that Marcy needed to attend. Madame Diversity would do anything to get her granddaughter out of the Jewish school. And using Mule Slides might postpone a conversation (or confrontation) with my errant, estranged husband. *Hah.* I listened harder to pick up specific school names.

"We're on the list at St. X and St. Y. We passed on St. Z because I hear you just have to be a sib or a legacy to get in. I've been coaching Anne Marie for her interviews. Do you think she has to know her phone number?"

"I don't know. At ABC Prep you have two screenings, one with other children and one without. I'm more worried about how Cummings will do with the other kids."

"Are you really thinking about ABC Prep? It's so far away. And most of those kids stay there the whole time instead of going on to Plant High School. I just can't imagine my little Michael Thomas going to high school anywhere but Plant. Or maybe Jesuit."

"Only ten minutes for us. But we're also looking at St. Z. Cummings' daddy went there. Bryn told me at Junior League the other day that she's sending Birch there too. Birch is a legacy, just like Cummings."

"Ooh, lucky dogs."

"Luck is only a part of it. Cummings' granddaddy has donated some new playground equipment and I've been attending services there for two years."

"I didn't know you were Episcopalian."

"I am now."

When it seemed a little too awkward to keep up the imaginary child ruse, I walked away from the play area and stopped for a coffee at Starbucks. I pulled out my notepad and jotted down a few notes about what I'd learned. I made a few broad generalizations:

- All women in South Tampa were formerly teachers, educated at southeastern schools
- All women in South Tampa attend bible study
- All women in South Tampa send older kids to summer camp
- School age kids go to St. Whatever-so-long-as-it's-south-of-Kennedy

- All South Tampa kids have two first names, or names that sound like last names.
- Most South Tampa women are some shade of blonde
- Remember to check out Junior League.

16. Birds and Bees

After Marcy got home from school, I phoned Mule Slides and found her unusually cooperative on the subject of Marcy's school for next year. She would make some phone calls and donations (and threats, most likely). I turned my attention to a little housekeeping while Marcy entertained herself.

I kicked an empty moving box over to the bookshelves in the family room. Jeff had crammed most of the shelves with his highbrow literature and business-school books. My books about art history, color theory and impressionism were stacked on the bottom shelf along with a collection of Marcy's chewed-up board books. I swept Jeff's collection into the cardboard box and regarded the empty shelf space with my most artistic eye. I desired to collect an impressive book collection of my own, perhaps based on Oprah's old book club. In the meantime, I would have to fill the space with displays of another sort.

I wandered upstairs into the room we used as an office. I found some dusty boxes of personal junk that had never been unpacked. I was looking for my old collection of framed postcards. Jeff hadn't ever let me put them out at our other house, never mind at this new one. I'd bought them all myself and I thought they were kind of campy. Looking in the top box, I didn't find the cards but I did run across my wedding album.

I flipped quickly through the pages. A hard pain settled in my chest as I looked at the pictures of Jeff and me with our cheesy smiles and hopeful demeanors. We had been married for seven years. After college, while Jeff had pursued a consulting career, I'd worked as an office assistant and receptionist at a large shoe manufacturing company. I had hoped to move into the company's art department at some point. The company did a lot of its own ad campaigns. But my single-minded pursuit of that ambition had lost its importance when Marcy was born. I had simply insisted that I be a stay at home mom. So we'd managed our money closely, moved to Tampa for a fresh start, and had lived off Jeff's car sales income ever since.

The pain in my chest eased slightly. *Used car salesman.* Before, marrying Jeff had seemed like a step up in society. My own parents had toiled for years as janitors in the local school system. *Admittedly low on the status totem pole.* Before my mother had made her surprise move to Tampa, I hadn't seen her or my father very often. I hated visiting my hometown and my parent's home. Their house always stank like hospital antiseptics because my father was something of a hypochondriac. Even if his imagined illnesses were not contagious, I wasn't so sure that you couldn't catch hypochondria. So I'd just sent them pictures of Marcy twice a year.

Now Jeff, my Knight in Shining Armor, was a used car salesman (never mind lying cheater) — the subject, if not the punch line, of countless jokes.

Just then, Marcy waltzed into the room with her pants pulled down around her ankles.

"Hi Mommy."

"Hi Marce. What are you doing?" I tried not to laugh.

"What's down there?" Marcy pointed at her crotch.

"Uhm, people call that part of your body the crotch."

"So only girls have crotches?"

"No, Honey." I helped Marcy pull up her pants, stalling for time to think up an explanation.

"Boys have crotches? Where their pee-pees are?"

"Yes. Boys and girls have crotches."

"But girls don't have pee-pees. What's down there?" Marcy looked tearful and intense. I finally understood.

"Marcy, boys have *penises*. That's what you may have seen on Daddy when he goes potty. Remember how we told you that boys can go pee-pee standing up?"

Marcy looked extremely exasperated. "MOMMY! WHAT'S DOWN THERE ON ME?" she yelled at the top of her little voice.

I explained in vague and hurried terms the various anatomical differences between boys and girls, reminding Marcy that she was free to refer to the whole thing in general terms, like crotch. Marcy decided to refer to her backside as her bottom and her front side as her utsey. I didn't object. At the time I couldn't even remember the word, "vulva." This solution satisfied Marcy who went back to play wherever she'd come from. I smiled at the memory of those early days when Marcy had been nothing more than a little meatloaf, eating, pooping and unable to smile back at us. Time flies. *Thank goodness*. In those early days, I had been somewhat depressed and isolated at home with my beautiful daughter. Most of my old friends had backed off when I got married. They had remained single long after I wed. To my old single friends, babies had been incomprehensible, some vague concept to be addressed later, after landing the perfect sperm donor (a.k.a. rich man). So I had felt very alone with my baby, my baby paraphernalia, and my prescription for Prozac.

Jeff had finally moved the whole family to Tampa for a fresh start, with the hopes that Ol' Mule Slides would prove more helpful than my parents had been. The jury was still out. I regarded a picture of Jeff's mom in the album. *Wow, she hadn't changed one bit in seven years. Was she born looking like she had an irritable bowel?* I chuckled when I remembered how Jeff used to characterize his mother: a complicated woman with uncomfortable shoes, a distaste for fun, and a penchant for sprinkling hot sauce on her eggs. Tall, lean and cranky, Mrs. Pintoff-Dower was not somebody to be toyed with. Even Marjorie hadn't made any mention of visiting my in-law.

I put away the album and decided to run to the grocery store with Marcy. Redecorating could wait. There were too many distractions in the way. Better to go buy some snack food. And a bottle of vitamins. Besides, Marjorie would just rearrange everything again when she returned from the beach with Kate, who had dragged her out to Clearwater Beach to try parasailing or something equally dangerous and stupid. Since she'd arrived, Kate hadn't so much as offered to baby-sit, let alone look for a job.

I baited Marcy with the promise of a cookie at the grocery store. As we strolled up and down the aisles, Marcy queried each shopper with the same question: "What's in *your* crotch?"

I just faced straight ahead and pushed the cart. Telling Marcy *not* to ask that question would beg the opposite result. *Ignore, ignore, ignore.*

17. Not for Lack of Grace

With Marcy in school, it was easier for me to spy on Weed Lady, a pastime that threatened to become an obsession now that I had a little free time on my hands and the motivation to get out of the house and away from my mother. Today, in an effort to discover Weed Lady's name, I planned to investigate Weed Lady's mail. I had mailed a card to Margaret from my own mailbox that morning so that when the little red flag was down, I'd know that the mailman had been there. As I pulled into my driveway, I smiled to see the little flag in the horizontal position. *Mail call.*

I felt bold. I had a foolproof plan. I would collect my own mail, act surprised, look around the neighborhood, and walk over to open Weed Lady's mailbox as if the mail carrier had wrongly delivered a piece of mail. Simple. Clean.

I left my purse in my car and headed over to get my mail. I glanced around first to make sure nobody was out in his or her yard. The coast was clear. I gathered my mail: a Good Housekeeping magazine, several bills, some credit card solicitations, and a thick stack of junk. Holding up a small, windowed envelope, I conveyed a look of concern and looked thoughtfully up and down the street, locating Weed Lady's address on her mailbox post. I walked deliberately over to Weed Lady's mailbox, and after happily noting that Weed Lady's car was not in the curved drive, I opened it up and pretended to place my bill in the mailbox.

Inside, I found a large stack of mail. Every piece was addressed to Grace Swingler, Ms. G. Swingler, Ms. Grace Swingler or Current Resident, Gracie Swingler, and in one instance, Grack Spingler. Not one piece of mail mentioned a Mister Swingler. So, Weed Lady's name was Grace and she was indeed single.

I took back my piece of mail and strolled home, trying to digest this information. Since Weed Lady, scratch that, *Grace's*, house was not directly in view from my windows, I hadn't paid that much attention to who was coming and going from the Swingler house, until very recently, of course. I had assumed that everybody on the block was married with children. I'd lately assumed that Jeff had taken up with a married woman as a sort of dalliance. A heinous, spiteful, awful dalliance, but a dalliance nevertheless. If Grace was single, that fact somehow made the possibility more real that Jeff was simply moving on with the first single, grabby bitch he could find.

How could he be moving on already? Wasn't he planning to work things out with me, at least for the sake of Marcy? Tears made a surprise appearance on my lashes and cheeks. I angrily brushed them away. For the past couple of days when I'd dared allow myself to consider what might be going on between Jeff and my neighbor, I'd really believed Margaret's assessment that Jeff was having a little flirtation (okay, affair) with a married neighbor and that sooner or later he'd either get dumped by her or beaten up by her husband, and then he'd come crawling back to me. I'd never been able to decide what would happen next, exactly, but I'd always envisioned Jeff trying to get the two of us back together. Now a new word was worming its way into my consciousness: *abandoned*.

Before I could slip up my driveway and into my house, Twin Vans called to me from across the street. I dabbed furiously at my eyes but unfortunately, even expensive make-up counter mascara runs under the weight of tears.

"Janice, hi. How are you doing?" Twin Vans walked across the street towards me. She had on her usual finery.

I was alarmed by the tone of Twin Vans' voice. It showed concern before she could possibly have noticed my tears. *She knows*!

"Actually, I heard about you and Jeff." Twin Vans face was screwed up into what must pass for a compassionate look when your face is numbed by Botox. "Is that your mom who came to live with you?"

Bingo. I tried a non sequitur. "I accidentally got a piece of Grace's mail."

Twin Vans followed this train of conversation. "You know, I'm always getting the strangest things in my mailbox, but fortunately not anybody else's mail. Not yet anyway. Yesterday I got a piece of mail addressed to Francis Sturch. Frances with an 'i'. As if a male would be subscribing to Good Housekeeping. Ha, ha, ha." She seemed beyond uncomfortable.

Frances Sturch. Now I knew the names of two of my neighbors. And I knew that Twin Vans and I both subscribed to Good Housekeeping. "So what exactly did you hear about me and Jeff, Frances?" I felt calmer. I put back on my game face.

"Actually, Grace told me that you two were separated or something. I just couldn't believe it. I guess I just don't like to believe anything until I hear it from the horse's mouth."

Right. I knew better. In the first few minutes before Marcy had puked at my December brunch, I had learned that my neighbors liked nothing better than gossip. "Well, neigh, neigh."

Ms. Frances Twin Vans didn't know how to react. She backed off, having gained the confirmation she was looking for, and gave a noncommittal, "If there's anything I can do . . ."

"You can save your leftovers for me and Marcy."

Frances widened her eyes but I cut her off before she could say anything.

"Kidding, Frances. We're fine. Fine and dandy, cotton candy, as Marcy likes to say." I started to back away too. "We'll really have to do lunch sometime, Frances with an 'e.'"

"Yes, lunch, well, I rarely eat that. But anyway, well, goodbye." Frances sped away up her path. I felt sure that Twin Vans was going to call up her telephone grapevine and spread the news about Jeff and me. A*t least I'm interesting enough to be talked about.*

With new resolve not to get derailed by Jeff's behavior, or Twin Van's for that matter, I retreated to my house and made a picnic lunch for Marcy. I was going to pick Marcy up from school and take her to the park. Kate Jackson Park. Marcy and I still ate lunch.

18. Super Ego

Kate, Marjorie and I ate in silence, as if we couldn't bear to miss one moment of the play-by-play streaming out of the television. Since Marcy was spending Super Bowl Sunday at Jeff's house, Marjorie had decided that the three of us needed to have a Super Bowl party. She'd "cooked" up raw chili by mixing a bunch of crudités with a few cans of dark red kidney beans and a little Tabasco sauce. Then she'd baked a football shaped apple cake and written "Go Team" with raisins on the icing. She looked very pleased with her handiwork although she admitted to having some minor discomfort watching television on a Sunday. Guru Ted had told her to set aside Sundays as a day of calm reflection and self-nurturing. Marjorie had invited Margaret to join us but it didn't take a rocket scientist or a financial manager to figure out that the party was going to be a tension-filled dud. Margaret had declined.

In the month since Kate and Marjorie had landed on my doorstep, Kate had taken our mother's car everyday to the beach or the lake or the mall or the dog park or wherever lazy, tattooed twenty-somethings went to avoid responsibility. It was really getting on my nerves and as usual, I blamed my mom. If Marjorie would just go back to New York, or anywhere else, I could regain control of the situation.

Unfortunately, Marjorie was thoroughly entrenched in my house. She'd even wall-papered the guest room without so much as asking my advice on color and design. I had managed to talk to my dad a few times on the phone but he'd always claimed to be too ill to discuss anything other than his latest aches and the weather. It didn't appear that he was going to be a useful ally in this situation. In fact, he was talking a lot lately about his home health care nurse, a pretty fifty year old with a son in Detroit.

So far as I knew, my mother and father had not spoken since my mother left him. She did speak occasionally to her spiritual mentor, Ted, and had recently begun practicing Tai Chi in the back yard. It was a little embarrassing but I looked on the bright side, at least my mom hadn't been bringing home dates. Her sexual orientation had failed to develop as an issue and of course, I attributed that fact to my own open-mindedness. I was perfectly okay with my mom being gay for a while so long as I didn't have to see it.

Now, as I crunched on a raw carrot, I tried to focus on what action I could take to regain control of my own house. Unable to simply speak my mind, I began criticizing the food.

"Mom, aren't canned beans cooked before they're canned?" I asked.

"I think so. Why?"

"So this is actually 'semi-raw' chili that we're eating? I just wanted to make sure I had it straight. Your dietary rules are hard to follow. How do you handle ceviche? "

Marjorie didn't respond so Kate jumped in. "You shouldn't pick on mom so much, Janice. It's not like you were going to cook anything tonight."

"You're a good one to talk, Miss Industrious," I responded. "When are you going to get a job, anyway?"

"When are *you* going to get a job?"

"I *have* a job taking care of Marcy. And you and Mom, from the looks of things."

"Oooh, that's a lot. You should ask for a raise."

"Girls! Please, we're missing the commercials. Talk when the boys are banging into each other."

Kate and I laughed. "Mom, really, enough with the raw food," I implored.

"The cake is cooked, but only because I draw the line at raw eggs."

"You're pretty loose with the laws, Mom. Ted's going to chant you into a coma or something."

"It never hurts to be adaptable, Janice. That goes for you too, Kate."

"Great mom, way to get all serious. And I was the one sticking up for you." Kate abruptly departed leaving most of her food and the iced tea she'd been drinking. Marjorie and I heard the car start up in the driveway.

"Must be PMS. I hope she pays you for the gas," I stated.

"That's none of your business, dear," Marjorie responded and the two of us watched television in silence until the team in blue won the game. I went to bed without wondering where my sister had gone. I was newly energized about my business plan. Kate was right. I *did* need a job, but not working for somebody else. Once my little consulting business was on a roll, I could consider evicting my relatives. I'd do it now but I'd already grown a little dependent on the money my mom was slipping me on the side. As I drifted off to sleep, it felt good to focus on myself and leave the worries about my mom, my sister, and my philandering husband behind. Of course I had taken one quick peek up the street to see if Jeff was watching the game at Weed Lady's house.

Nope.

19. Giraffes *Do* Talk

By mid-February, my business research was well underway. I spoke about it to Margaret one morning on my cell phone while I drove Marcy to school.

"Your friend Trudy has been really helpful, Mags. Thanks for giving me her number. We're having our first meeting early next month. She's really anxious to hear what I have to say, and that's quite a lot, I'm proud to admit."

"Ah, ma petite parvenue."

"What's a parvenue?"

"You. Look it up in Marcy's dictionary. Where are you, anyway?"

"I'm taking Marcy to school."

"What are you doing after? Want to come by?"

I had an urge to pretend I'd lost my connection. Instead I begged off to do mommy errands. Margaret would understand.

"So I'll call you next week, okay?" I got off the phone with Margaret and smiled at Marcy in the back seat. Marcy was uncharacteristically quiet because she was pretending to be Dopey the dwarf from Snow White. Dopey can't talk.

"Hey, Dopey, can you wiggle your gears, I mean, ears for me?" Marcy grabbed her ears and flapped them for me. I was playing the part of Doc. Then Marcy broke her silence.

"Oh no! The wicked queen just put a spell on us and now Dopey can talk and Doc is a giraffe."

In other words, Marcy was tired of being quiet. Now it was my turn to be silent. Giraffes don't talk either. That was fine with me. I drove in silence through the tree-lined neighborhoods where the usual morning exchange was taking place. Dads were in sedans on their way to work and moms were in minivans and SUVs on their way to school drop-offs. They were fleeing the neighborhoods while the workers flooded in: lawn care companies, tree services, construction workers, house painters, delivery trucks, garbage haulers, nannies, etc. The people who were paid to be there got to spend a lot more daytime in these beautiful neighborhoods than the homeowners. *Sad.*

At drop-off, I parked the car and tugged the now very chatty Dopey into the school. "Honey, why don't you pretend to be Marcy now. We'll be dwarfs again later, okay?"

"Shhhh! Giraffes don't talk."

I rolled my eyes and spotted the person I'd worn my best new slacks and twin set for: Gregory Storm, Lucas's dad. Lucas Storm's friendly, affluent, hot as shit, single dad. Heart rate rising, I blushed and felt grateful to Gregory Storm for taking my mind off of the Jeff and Weed Lady thing, if only for the moment. We hadn't yet exchanged words or anything, but Lucas was in Marcy's class and it was only a matter of time. Funny enough, Marcy seemed to be developing a little crush on Lucas. She spoke about him non-stop when she deigned to speak of preschool rather than pretending to be a short, decidedly non-precocious cartoon movie character.

Today, Marcy broke the ice for me. "Mommy, MOMMY! That's Lucas." Marcy grabbed my hand and dragged me over to meet Lucas Storm, a handsome little boy with a collared shirt and scuffed sneakers.

"Hi, I'm Janice Darcy, when I'm not being a giraffe." I held my hand out to Lucas's dad. "I'm Marcy's mom."

Gregory Storm dazzled me with a smile and a warm, firm handshake. "So this is the famous Marcy?" He patted Marcy on the head. "We've been hearing a lot about Marcy around the house lately. Lucas made his older brother write out her name last night on a napkin."

"I guess the infatuation is mutual. Marcy told me that she and Lucas were going to grow up to be a mommy and daddy that go to work together. I should warn you that she thinks Lucas is going to be a construction worker who hammers nails all day."

"A chip off the old block. I own a construction company."

Oops. I managed to stave off another blush. I'd been a little condescending about the construction industry just then. Why had I assumed that Gregory Storm was Doctor Storm, or something like that? *Shame, shame.*

"So I guess we'll have to get the kids together for a play date sometime?" I tried to look just the slightest bit coy.

"That would be terrific. Lucas would love that." Gregory was all smiles and laughs. "Just promise me that they won't run off to Vegas."

"Ah, ha, ha." Snort. *Damn.* "I'll call you when I have my calendar in front of me." I knew damn well that there was nothing on my calendar but that was not something you advertised.

"Terrific. Thanks!"

We walked the kids into the classroom and departed at the same time so I was able to discern that Gregory Storm drove a Mercedes. *Mmmm.* Time to go clothes shopping.

Time to get a wax job. Time to sell Aunt Sally's antique buffet for some badly needed capital. Mom wouldn't care; Sally had been Dad's sister.

Time to get my business off the ground.

PART II: FEMME d'AFFAIRES
(Why is it even called "work"?)

YOU'RE INVITED

TO: A Bible Study Brunch

WHERE: Janice Darcy's House

WHEN: Wednesday, March10
                                  10:00 am

BRING: A Notebook

RSVP: 555-6871

20. Session One

I looked in the mirror and winked at myself. No closet game today. I inventoried my look: Lilly Pulitzer cropped pants; Lilly Pulitzer sleeveless cable-knit sweater; Ann Taylor sandals; French manicure; French pedicure; pearl earrings from Alvin Magnon; tiny gold cross pendant from the jewelry counter at Saks; Laura Mercier make-up (another couple hundred dollars spent in the search for the perfect make-up); nicely arched eyebrows; and perfectly coifed hair a la . . . okay, Fastclips, but I was working on that. The hair artists, or whatever they called themselves, at Fancy Clancy hadn't returned any of my messages. I'd nearly elected to wear an old cameo from my Aunt Sally but luckily, the most recent People magazine had informed me that cameos were passé. A Town & Country article at the dentist's office had said exactly the opposite, but who read that magazine?

I was nervous but I expected complete success this morning. I had tucked all thoughts about that first brunch three months ago under some rug in my brain. A lot had changed since then. For one thing, I, strike that, *Marcy*, had a play date with the Storm boy after school today. *Stop digressing — think about that later*. I was quickly becoming an expert, or so I thought, on the ins and outs of South Tampa. I was going to provide for these ladies the information I had so desperately needed myself when I'd first arrived on the scene. I was providing a necessary public service (albeit not a free one.)

I had the place to myself thanks to Marcy's school, Marjorie's bonsai club meeting, and Kate's new boyfriend, Gus. He was a rock and roll back up guitarist for the headliner at some hole near the beach. They were working on their tans and some lyrics for his breakout album. At least Kate was working part-time now waiting tables at the same bar where Gus played.

I descended the stairs lightly, inhaling the scent of ginger wafting up from the candle in the powder room. In the kitchen, pumpkin scones from The Bakery and a fruit plate from The Grocer's sat on display near a freshly brewed pot of Starbuck's coffee. I checked the time — ten o'clock. I'd arranged for Marcy to stay at school for lunch so that I would have plenty of time for my guests.

Three women were due to arrive at any moment: Trudy, Sandy, and Pat. Trudy was Margaret's friend from Lutz who had recently moved into Sunset Park, a neighborhood just south of Beach Park, my neighborhood. Sandy and Pat were friends of Trudy's, whose husbands worked in the same company as Trudy's husband. The entire company office had relocated to the Westshore business district and so many of the families were relocating, or planning to relocate soon to South Tampa. *Perfect.*

Trudy arrived first.

"Hi, you must be Trudy! It's so nice to meet you in person finally. I recognize you because Margaret told me you had beautiful red hair. Come in, come in."

"Thank you. It's nice to meet you too. Wow, what a beautiful home you have."

"Thank you," I responded demurely. I invited Trudy to come in and sit down in the living room, still painted Ralph Lauren's Mexican Feather Grass. The furnishings were still sparse but I had hung a myriad of black and white photos of Marcy on the wall. Most of them had been taken in the last month at the playground and at the beach. In the black frames with white mattes, they looked very artistic. A deep red couch ran the length of the room and two easy chairs in matching designer fabric completed the comfortable conversation area. *My new home office. Thank God for good credit.* I'd forbidden Marjorie from working her feng shui "magic" in this room.

Sandy and Pat soon arrived and when they were all settled with small plates of food and piping hot coffee, I began. Having vetted these clients as best I could (a phone call with Margaret), I was informed about their flush financial situations. So I addressed the financial details first.

"Welcome. As you all know, this isn't really a Bible study group. That's just our cover for discretion's sake. Not that studying the Bible is bad or anything. Ha, ha." I noticed the unchanged expressions on my guests' faces and moved right along. "I've gotten to know Trudy fairly well over the phone in the last couple of weeks and I'm sure she explained how this is going to work. The consultation fees need to be paid in advance for the session. Each session is six weeks long with meetings each week, and maybe a few field trips. And that's about it. This meeting is, of course, a freebie, to see if this arrangement will be mutually beneficial."

I paused to assess the initial reaction. They were all three listening very carefully to me, shifting occasionally to get more comfortable or wipe off a few crumbs. I took the lap shifting and napkin dabbing as subtle signs of excitement. I felt encouraged.

"Okay, then. I thought we'd start with appearances. After all, they make the first impression and in many ways, are the easiest to change. Oh, not that you all don't look great. It's just, well, here." I grabbed a small pile of handouts. "I've compiled a list of fashion labels and stores you should become familiar with, if you aren't already." I knew already that they were not well acquainted with my recommended brands. The three women were too casually dressed in khakis and white tee shirts. And their shoes were altogether too comfortable looking. These women reminded me of my former self. Diamonds in the rough.

I sneezed. "Sorry, the oak pollen is really getting to me today. Only in the South do leaves fall this time of year. My poor daughter is completely seasonally dysfunctional. She thinks it's autumn. Ha, ha." Nothing. Better drop the comedy act.

I passed around the lists neatly printed on colored paper. "I've color coded my topics. You'll notice that the lists pertaining to clothes are printed on pink. That's to remind you about the Pink Grotto, your first shopping stop after you leave my house." I chuckled lightly as I gestured at my pants and sweater. A knock at the door stole my attention.

"Oh, that must be my surprise! While I go answer the door, look over the non-disclosure statement and sign it for me. It's just a promise to keep things quiet. Naturally, it's in everyone's best interest that we keep our meetings and discussions discreet."

I flitted to the front door to admit a young woman with a small green case. I motioned her into the living room. "Everybody, this is Marta. She's studying to be a nail technician and I've invited her here to give manicures to my *Bible study* group. I guess while she's doing everyone's nails we can go ahead and eat some more and get to know each other. We'll get right back to business when Marta's done." I winked at my guests and sat down.

The manicurist started with Trudy. If Marta the manicurist thought that there was anything odd about having manicures at a Bible study meeting, she didn't let it show.

I soaked up the pleased expressions on the faces of my guests. Pat and Sandy exclaimed over the scones. Two hours later, my three guests departed with gleaming nails and I held three checks in the nervous palm of my hand. I was in business.

"Bye everyone. See you next week. Don't forget to get those pedicures before sandal season!" I waved to my departing clients. I waved again when I saw Twin Vans pull into her driveway across the street.

Twin Vans got out of her car and glanced at her own front door as if to assess the merits of a quick getaway. Instead she played the part of the neighborly neighbor. I did too.

"Hi Fran-cess," I exclaimed with heavy emphasis on the short "e" sound. "What's shakin'? Fall in a vat of green dye?" Twin Vans was wearing Kelley green from head to toe. She sported a jaunty green bowler on her head. A small wiener dog yapped in the front seat of her van.

"Hmmm, funny. Actually I was at a Junior League function for St. Patrick's Day," Twin Vans remarked without emotion. "Janice, I see you had company this morning. I just wanted to remind you that it's very difficult for me to get in and out of my driveway when there are cars parked on the street. Maybe you could have your guests park around the corner or something."

So, Twin Vans wasn't being neighborly. "Great idea. I'll let my Bible study group know for next time. I'm sure it's very awkward to maneuver those big giant cars of yours."

"Don't you drive a van?"

"Oh, yes I do have *one*. But I guess I just don't have any trouble driving it."

"I *don't* have trouble driving my . . . forget it. Have a nice day, Janice. I'm glad to hear you're attending Bible study. I'm sure you'll benefit." Twin Vans huffed her way back up her driveway and into her front door.

I wondered only briefly if I had just been put down. I also thought about waiting in Twin Van's driveway until she was forced to come out and retrieve her dog. No time. I was due to pick up Marcy for that play date.

21. Family Values

"I did it! I pulled it off!" I exclaimed into the cell phone as I lightly bumped the car in front of me with the van's front bumper. "Oops, I'll call you right back, Mags."

The owner of the station wagon was a tiny old lady who had slammed on the brakes the minute the light turned from green to yellow. I approached her with a smile. Our cars had barely touched each other. "Hi, I'll check the cars," I said.

The lady looked scared and didn't respond. She was still getting out of her vehicle. I looked at our bumpers. No detectable damage. "It all looks fine, ma'am. You don't even need to get out of your car."

The lady paused, uncertain. I noticed the Michigan license plate. *Had she driven all that way?* "I said it all looks fine, ma'am. We can go." The lady looked frozen in place. "MA'AM," I yelled, "OUR CARS ARE FINE. IF YOU LEAVE NOW, I WON'T TELL THE POLICE THAT YOU BROKE THE LAW. IN FLORIDA, YOU'RE SUPPOSED TO ACCELERATE THROUGH A YELLOW LIGHT!"

The people in the car behind me laughed as I had hoped they would. I felt like having an audience. The lady climbed back into her car and sped off. I continued on my way to pick up Marcy, hitting redial on my phone. Margaret was at work.

"So you are now talking to a successful, self-employed businesswoman on my way to fetch my successful, brilliant child. We have a date with the Storm boys this afternoon."

"Ma petite femme d'affaires! I'm so proud of you."

"Margaret, I'm not having an affair!"

Margaret laughed. "It doesn't mean that."

"Well quit speaking French. This is America, last time I checked. Anyway, you're spoiling my mood."

"Sounds like nothing could spoil it. So your first session went well, I take it."

"Perfect."

"And Mr. Storm is on the agenda for this afternoon?"

"Also perfect."

"What are you wearing?"

"Sleeveless sweater and cropped pants. I look great."

"I'm sure you do. Of course, if you would ever come over, I'd know first hand. I haven't seen you forever. I see your mom more than you. She's here now. Do you want to talk to her?"

"What's she doing there?"

"Shopping I would guess. It is a clothing store. She said she'd been banished from your house."

I felt a little guilty. I *had* banished my mom and I *had* been ducking Margaret. "Tell her she's welcome to go home but if she has any of those little trees with her, tell her to leave them somewhere that Marcy can't reach them or they might get decorated with doll clothes and plastic bugs. Hey gotta run, I'm at the school. Let's get together soon."

Margaret didn't press for a date. "See you Janice. Let me know how the play date goes."

I retrieved Marcy from the school and headed directly home. It wasn't until I'd pulled in my driveway that I noticed Ol' Mule Slides on my front step.

"Grandma!" Marcy yelled as she got out of the car and dashed across the grass. Mule Slides held a gift bag in her hand.

"Hello. Won't you come in?" I asked without enthusiasm. In the three months since Jeff had moved, Mule Slides hadn't once set foot in my house. She occasionally had Marcy over for a visit but even more often she stopped by unannounced with little treasures for Marcy that she wanted to drop off. Little Christian treasures. Today it was a book about the story of Noah in cutesy rhymes.

"You know, Mrs. Dower, they do teach the story of Noah at Marcy's school. They're Jewish, not godless."

"Yes, well, it doesn't hurt for my grandchild to hear the Christian version. I was just out for a walk and in your part of the neighborhood . . ."

Stalking my house, no doubt. I had noticed that she always managed to stop in when Marjorie was away. Marjorie's car was still missing from the driveway. How had Jeff turned out so normal? Mule Slides must have given him a lot to overcome. Early in our marriage, Mule Slides had told me the "funny" story about the two men she'd eavesdropped on in a checkout line. The black man had been talking to the other, a white man, about their work schedule when it had become obvious that the white man was actually the black man's assistant. Imagine! I hadn't said anything at the time. Pointing out your mother-in-law's bigotry usually comes later in the relationship. I was lucky that I'd held my tongue. Mule Slides had followed up her story by giving Jeff and me tickets to an event called The Fruit Ball, a celebration honoring some man she'd supported in his bid to become a new member of the Florida senate.

The Ball had provided me with my first taste of Tampa society. It was years ago, before we'd even moved to Tampa, but I still thought about it. Weddings aside, it was the only black tie event I'd ever been to. I'd worn a beautiful dress in a soft green, the same color all the bridesmaids had worn to Mindy Colton's wedding. Hers was the one wedding in which I had participated. Jeff had rented a tuxedo for the Ball. It had been catered by one of the best-known restaurants in town with music provided by a small jazz ensemble. The highest point in the evening had been when the brother-in-law of the Mayor had asked me to dance. Prior to that, I'd spent the entire evening standing next to Jeff, swaying and tapping and wishing Jeff knew how to dance. When I'd finally received my invitation, I hadn't even looked at Jeff to see if he approved or not. Come on, it was the Mayor's brother-in-law! In the ensuing years, the Fruit Ball had become a yearly charity event that all the socialites attended. I hoped to score an invitation on my own merits soon.

"Thank you, Mrs. Dower. I'll read this to Marcy tonight. But we have to get going. She's got a play date today."

Mule Slides knelt down uneasily on the front step and placed a kiss on Marcy's forehead. Her ankles tottered in the high heeled slip-ons she was wearing today, a sporty pair with stacked rubber soles and two white stripes. Running mules? "Bye-bye, little one. I'll see you soon. Grandma loves you."

I didn't offer her a ride home.

Once inside, I scurried around after Marcy, picking up discarded shoes and socks and empty juice boxes.

"Lucas will be here soon to play so let's not mess up the house, okay?"

"Can I watch a kid's show?"

"Sure, Marcy. Let's see what's on." The television would provide some excellent babysitting right at the moment. A message on the answering machine informed me that Marjorie and Margaret were going to be having dinner together later and that Marjorie would be home after that. I felt a little squirmy at the news and didn't want to examine where that feeling was coming from. My sister had started referring to Marjorie and Margaret as M&M. They had been spending a lot of time together. *Ick, don't even think it*. No time to ponder that question anyway, the Storms were due at any minute.

22. Play Date

The black Mercedes pulled into my driveway at precisely three o'clock. *Prompt, I like that.* Gregory Storm wore a big smile as he fished Lucas out of the back seat. He waved towards me as I stared out the front window. He was wearing faded jeans and an expensive looking long-sleeved shirt. His feet were clad in brown shoes like the ones people wear when they want to look like they go yachting on weekends. In his case, it could very well be true. A brief fantasy flashed through my mind: I was holding the rail on a large sailboat, the wind was whipping through my hair, and my sweater had a nice nautical stripe to match my cropped pants and pristine white sneakers. Was that sea salt I smelled? *Mmmm.*

I met them at the front door. "Hi guys. Oh Lucas, Marcy will be so pleased to see you." I turned and yelled up the stairs, "MARCY!" I was still wearing the outfit from my morning brunch and I felt unusually confident and attractive. Even my bathroom scale had cooperated with me this morning. I was down two pounds since the weekend.

Marcy came sheepishly down the stairs. She was clutching a toy electric drill out of the set of tools I had bought in anticipation of this play date. Marcy didn't otherwise have a lot of toys you usually associate with little boys. I waved for Marcy to hurry down the stairs and turned back to the Storms.

Gregory Storm held out his hand. "Nice to see you again, Janice. It's really nice of you to have Lucas over. He's pretty excited, aren't you, Luke?" Gregory Storm roughed his palm over Lucas's blond head.

"Well, come in," I stood back from the door. "I've got some snacks for the kids and I made a little something special for us grown-ups."

At the very same time, Gregory Storm spoke to his son. "I'll be back around five, Luke." Gregory looked up at me, "That's okay, isn't it? Oh, what? You made something?"

I kept the smile frozen on my face as I glanced from Gregory to Lucas to the black Mercedes. There was somebody else in it but thanks to the darkly tinted windows, I couldn't make out anything about the person. Probably another woman. I had not realized that this was going to be a drop-off play date. A drop-off play date was not at all what I'd had in mind. Who had drop-off play dates with three and a half year olds? *Who the hell had said anything about a drop-off play date?*

"Well, five o'clock is just fine, Gregory, and yes, I did make something for us, you. Wait here." My manic smile and I disappeared into the kitchen. A fresh loaf of pumpkin bread sat out on a special serving plate with a small dish of butter and two fancy dessert plates. Coffee was brewing in the pot near the sink. I grabbed a large plastic bag from a drawer and slid the entire loaf of bread into it. I closed it with a twisty thing and rushed back out to the front door.

Still smiling, I presented Gregory with the pumpkin bread. "Just a little something I whipped up this morning. Two loaves are too much for me and Marcy so I thought I would share with you boys."

"That's really thoughtful," said Gregory as he glanced at his car. "I'll see you a little later."

"Uh hum, see you." My weird frozen smile didn't disintegrate until Gregory, his black Mercedes and his little chippy were long gone.

I noticed Twin Vans staring out her screen door. "See you very soon, Gregory," I trilled loudly enough for Twin Vans to hear before I went back into the house after the kids.

The next two hours crawled by. I ate most of the second loaf of pumpkin bread and all the butter while Marcy and Lucas played up in her room. *When are they too old to play alone with the door closed?* I watched the minutes tick by on my kitchen clock. I was upset with Gregory for having left but I was even more upset with myself for letting that fact depress me. It threatened to ruin my elation over this morning's successful business meeting. Before, it was Jeff who had squelched my enthusiasm. Was I going to let some guy I didn't even know have that kind of power over me? No fucking way. *Pardon my French.*

Gregory Storm returned promptly at five to retrieve his son. I couldn't tell if there was anyone else in the car and prided myself for the fact that I hadn't looked all that hard to see. "MARCY! LUCAS! Come on down, guys."

My smile was much more natural as I inquired if Gregory had had a nice afternoon.

"Sure. I had to take Lucas's big brother to the doctor. I can't think of anywhere I'd rather spend the afternoon than in a pediatrician's office with a bunch of runny nosed kids, exposing my son to God knows what. How did things go here?"

His son was sick. No chippy. Just a sick kid. Oh, poor sick kid. Yeah! No chippy! My smile broadened. "Oh, the afternoon was great. They've been playing in Marcy's room."

Just then Marcy and Lucas descended the stairs. Marcy was wearing a fake Hawaiian grass skirt over her days-of-the-week underpants and nothing else. *A cover off of National Geographic*? Lucas had on a full face of make-up, probably some of my expensive new products, and one of my slips pulled up to his armpits. Luckily, he was still wearing his clothes underneath the black satin.

"Hi Daddy," Lucas grinned through a clown's mouth. "We played dress up."

I was afraid to turn around. My face had to be bright crimson.

"Well, son, I see you've had a nice time here. Let's go, Jack is waiting in the car. Maybe you should leave the skirt here?"

"I have a wipe for his face, just a minute." I raced into the bathroom and grabbed a pre-moistened towelette. Why hadn't I checked on the children? Was it so bad that they dressed up? *Ugh*.

"Here you are, Lucas. You know, with your coloring, a pinker shade of lipstick might work better." *Please, please, please let Gregory Storm have a sense of humor*.

"You know, I have a nice shade of mauve at home you can try, buddy." Gregory Storm winked at me and escorted his son to the car. I was pretty sure that there wouldn't be any more play dates but a date of the other variety was definitely not out of the question.

23. Grace At Mealtime

I phoned Margaret later on my way to the pizza restaurant with Marcy. "Oh, God, you can't believe it. He was covered with make-up and he was wearing one of my slips. Marcy was half-naked."

"Didn't you check on them at all?"

"How was I supposed to know that the son of Mr. Testosterone would choose beauty products over plastic tools."

"Mr. Testosterone probably has a handy man on staff and little Lucas hasn't ever seen a drill before."

"Get out of here. Well, anyway, Gregory made a joke about it so I think things are okay. He might have even winked at me when he said it. God, Margaret, I feel like a high-school girl."

"Just don't write his name all over your book bag and you'll be fine. Do you think he'll ask you out?"

"Way too soon to tell. But trust me, I'll let you know. Say, where are you and mom meeting for dinner?"

"Some build-your-own salad place. You know your mom – it's all got to be raw."

"Yeah, right," I replied. "Well, you girls have a good time and be sure to have my mother home before eleven. Hah, hah."

"The boys have to be home long before that, dingbat."

"Oh, they're with you? So, okay, well I hope they like lettuce." I felt stupid and relieved. I bid Margaret goodbye and felt guilty, briefly, for not having thought to inquire about Margaret's dating status. After all, Margaret had been single a lot longer than me. *Am I single?* Goosebumps rose on my arms.

At the restaurant, I ordered a small cheese pizza with half of it covered in sausage and olives. Marcy and I sat at a large table near a window and were relatively quiet as we went about our work devouring the pizza. Marcy must have been starving to eat so quietly. Grease dripped down my fingers as I shoveled large bites into my mouth. Come to think of it, I was pretty hungry myself. A few small drips of oil spattered across my sweater. *Oh well.*

I had most of a slice crammed into my mouth when a strange, giggly voice asked to join us.

"Hi. I'm Grace, your neighbor across the street and down a couple of houses. Hee, hee. I'm so sorry I haven't been able to come over and introduce myself before. Do you mind if I join you?"

I gestured at an empty chair, my voice frozen in my throat. *This giggle-bag was Weed Lady? Was this some sort of joke?*

Weed Lady must have sensed my unease and focused on Marcy. "I'm Gracie. Do you like pizza, Marcy? I eat it all the time. Hee, hee."

Does Marcy like pizza? Doesn't she have a wad of cheese dripping off of her chin? I offered a greasy handshake. "Marcy's a purist. Cheese and sauce. I guess you know I'm Janice. Janice Darcy *Pintoff.*"

Weed Lady barely touched my hand and gave a sort of air-shake. "Thanks for letting me join you. I love their pizza here but I get tired of eating it by myself." Weed Lady nibbled at a sauce-less, cheese-less, vegetarian delight that looked nothing like a pizza at all. She looked up and giggled a couple of times at Marcy.

As Weed Lady, Marcy and I all chewed, I contemplated the situation and decided on a bold course of action. I didn't know why Weed Lady had been brazen enough to sit at our table – probably some game of her own – but I made the sudden decision to become Weed Lady's best friend and most-intrusive neighbor. *Wouldn't that drive Jeff entirely mad?* And I planned to make sure that Weed Lady knew all about my adventures in dating. Hopefully beginning with Gregory Storm. *Oh God, Margaret would be so proud.*

"So Grace, you just have to come over for coffee tomorrow while Marcy's at school. I want to get your opinion on some redecorating I'm doing. Your house looks so great, I figure you must have excellent taste."

"Oh, thanks! Hee, hee. I'd love to come have coffee before I go to work. Around nine?"

"Great!" I proceeded to eat the cheesy, saucy mess in front of me as Weed Lady finished maybe two bites and called it a night. "See you tomorrow then?"

"Mmmm."

After Weed Lady departed, I turned the conversation to Marcy but my thoughts were elsewhere. *What was Grace Swingler's game? Did Jeff put her up to this? Not at all likely. She probably thinks I couldn't possibly know about the two of them and she wants to find out some dirt about me. Well, I'm going to give her some. Ha, ha.* Snort. *Damn.*

"Are you done, Sweetie?"

"I'm Grumpy. Bah!"

"Are you finished, Grumpy? Snow White wants to go home to her castle and clean up."

"Hmmph. Bah."

"I'll let you skip your bath. I know Grumpy hates baths."

"Okay. And I want some apple juice."

"Done."

24. All Gussied Up

I came downstairs at seven in the morning to find Kate and Gus wrapped up in each other and an old blanket on the new red couch. Gus was snoring loudly.

"GET UP! Marcy will be down here any minute!" I furiously grabbed up various articles of clothing and flung them at the couch. "Jesus Christ," I exclaimed at the sight of an empty condom wrapper.

"Good morning to you too," Kate responded through dry lips and an obvious hangover. Gus snored on as Kate peeled herself off of him. "Do you have any aspirin?"

"You're lucky I came downstairs before Mom. She'd have a cow!"

"No she wouldn't. She's cool about sexuality. *You're* the one having a cow."

"Oh yes, Marjorie's cool. Now I know you're delusional." I handed the clothes to Kate. "You guys have to get out of here. I have company coming in a little while and I don't want to have to explain this to Marcy."

"Marcy'd be cool."

"Shut up, Kate. Get your clothes on and get him out of here."

"You shut up."

"What are you, three? This is the kind of conversation I have with Marcy."

"Right. You're *her* mother. Not mine. My mother wouldn't ever talk to me like this."

"Did we even grow up in the same house?"

Marjorie *had* found me in the clutches of an older boy one time after a high school play. We'd been kissing each other mostly because everybody else at the cast party had hooked up leaving us stranded in a sea of smoochy-face. I had liked the boy and it was only a kiss but Marjorie had grabbed me by the arm, dragged me from the house and wordlessly driven me home. Maybe Marjorie had planned to give me a verbal lashing, but if she had, her plan had been abandoned upon our arrival home. Dad had claimed to have a migraine and needed to get away from toddler Kate (then still Kathryn) and her relentless screaming. He'd left the house leaving Marjorie to comfort Kate who had been legitimately ill with a fever. I had been left alone. Looking back, I alternately condemned my mom for overreacting and for not reacting at all.

"We'll talk about this later," I said to Kate. *God, how had Marjorie screwed up so badly raising this one?*

Gus rolled over and sputtered awake. "Mornin' all. What time is it?" He checked his wrist for a non-existent watch.

"Hey Gussy, it's early but the woman of the house has declared us trespassers. Let's go to your place and have some breakfast." Kate shot me an ugly glance that I chose to ignore. Just as I ignored the latest tattoo on Kate's rear end – the word "Gus" in fancy script surrounded by a heart. *Gross.*

"Can't Darlin'" Gus replied. "I've got some business to attend to. Thanks for last night, though." He stood up, fully naked, and kissed Kate full on the lips.

"Oh my God, that's Marcy," I whisper-yelled as I heard a door open upstairs. "Get the fuck out of here!"

Gus gave some sort of knowing glance to Kate as he pulled on his shorts and collected the rest of his clothes. Kate walked him to the front door and gave him a *long* kiss goodbye. Then she lit into me.

"Thanks a fucking lot, big sister. I finally meet a decent guy and you work your usual magic."

"What does that even mean?"

Just then Marjorie descended the stairs with Marcy. "Look who I found," Marjorie exclaimed as they entered the room. She didn't wait for a reply, however, having seen the intense looks on her daughter's faces. *Did she even notice that her youngest daughter was stark naked?* "Marcy, let's you and I go make some breakfast. How do strawberries sound?"

"Nummy," Marcy answered as they headed toward the kitchen.

I squared off towards Kate. "What did that mean, 'my usual magic'?"

"You figure it out, Miss Brainy-Pants. I'm off to go screw up your life a little more. It's my job, as you seem to point out on a daily basis." Kate stomped up the stairs, her "Gus" tattoo jiggling behind her.

I yelled from the bottom of the stairs: "I just want you to have the opportunities that I missed out on. Go to college, have a career. Be yourself." *Don't be a tramp*, I added silently.

Kate turned towards me from the top of the stairs. "I am myself. I'm just not you. Sorry to disappoint."

Suddenly Marcy came dashing out from the kitchen with a strawberry in her hand. "Isn't this the most beautiful fruit berry you ever saw, Mommy?"

I couldn't speak, let alone respond with any alacrity. Kate disappeared into the guest room. "Mommy needs some coffee, honey, then I can look at your fruit, okay?" I followed Marcy back into the kitchen. I planned to load up on caffeine, have Marjorie drive Marcy to school, and then pick up any messes before Weed Lady/Grace came by for coffee. I'd deal with Kate later.

25. Coffee Break

Having entertained the day before, I had very little to do to get the house ready for Weed Lady's visit. I'd managed to whip up another loaf of pumpkin bread and brew fresh coffee. I'd also dashed out quickly to pick up a huge bouquet of red roses from the nearest florist. Very suggestive, I thought, although I'd winced at the credit card charge for the flowers. I'd been whipping that card out a lot lately. I placed the flowers in the living room. Next, my ruse about decorating advice needed to be addressed – maybe the upstairs bathroom. *Hello Grace, what color do you suggest for the room I poop in?* I decided not to be tacky in spite of the strong impulse. I adhered to the idea that it was better to foster kinship with the enemy. Weed Lady could look at the kitchen.

I met Grace walking up the driveway. "Hi there, Grace. Just said goodbye to my progeny. Come on in."

The front door stuck as I tried to open it but a quick shove with my shoulder did the trick.

Weed Lady followed me inside. "I'm anxious to see what you've done with the place. I knew the former owners. By the way, a little WD-40 might do the trick on that door."

Yes, Ms. Fix It. Did you sleep with the former master of the house too? "They seemed like nice folks. I only met them at the closing. Well, come on in. You know, I haven't lived here all that long so it's still a work in progress. I have been focusing on the front room. Why don't we sit in there and I'll get us some coffee. Do you take anything in it?"

"No, just black, thanks." Giggle.

I returned with a tray of pumpkin bread and two coffees. I set them down on the coffee table.

"Janice, your house looks really great. I really like that shade of green. It looks like a Farrow & Ball color."

"Oh, yes it is," I lied. "So anyway, would you like some pumpkin bread?"

"Sure. You don't usually get that this time of year. Did you use canned pumpkin?"

No, I froze a real pumpkin last Halloween and spent the last two days defrosting it and scraping it and peeling it and whatever else you might have to do with a pumpkin to make it look like the stuff you can so conveniently purchase in a can. Slut.

"Yes, but it was organic." *They make that, don't they?*

"It's delicious. So how are you and Marcy doing, anyway? I was so glad to run into you last night." Giggle, wink.

Winking now? That's new. "We're fine. You know. It's hard on Marcy – I assume you're talking about her father having moved, temporarily."

"Oh, is it just a temporary thing?"

What, no giggle? Did Grace look alarmed? Where was I going to go with this, anyway? "I guess time will tell, won't it."

"Sure, I understand. I hope everything works out for the best. For all of you. Jeff included. He's very likeable."

"So you've met?" I asked, noting that Grace did not say that she hoped Jeff and I got back together. *Double Slut.* Grace didn't even look uncomfortable. *Smooth.*

"Oh, yes. I'm sorry, I figured you knew."

"Oh, well, I . . ." I had not figured that we would actually discuss the affair. How could Grace even know that I knew? *Christ!*

"I bumped into him like three times at the mailbox when I was delivering some mail for you. I was collecting the mail before you moved in. Sorting it out for the family that moved. I think they belonged to three different dog clubs! Hee, hee."

So that's how it got started. No, Jeff hadn't mentioned it. Why would he? That also explains the state of the carpeting.

"New subject, Grace. Come look at my kitchen and tell me what you would do with it." I found that I couldn't discuss Jeff with this woman for one more second.

"I'd love to. Oh, before I forget, the reason I was so keen to meet you is that I thought you might like to join my book club. We're short a couple of members and I know you like to read."

"How do you know that?" I was surprised by the invitation.

"Your mail. There were some books you'd ordered. I'm sorry, have I said something wrong? You look a little upset."

Oops. "Of course not. I was just surprised. Yes, I would love to join a book club. When is your next meeting and what are you reading?"

"The next meeting is at my friend Lynne's house next Monday at seven o'clock. We're reading *Madame Bovary* by Flaubert."

Oh, a classic. La ti da. "I'll try to get it read before then. Actually, I think I probably read that back in high school. Thanks for thinking of me."

"Actually, I think of you often. I'm glad we got together. I'll get you directions to Lynne's." Giggle.

Triple Slut.

We proceeded into the kitchen where Grace gave her opinion about everything from the color, the need for a granite counter tops, and the brands of appliances I should consider. *Why hadn't I shown Grace the bathroom*? The kitchen makeover would be thousands of dollars. Better check "yes" on that latest pre-approved credit card offer.

26. Book Club

On Monday, I followed Grace's directions to Lynne Swanson's house. It was on Davis Island, close to downtown. I observed a mix of old, renovated houses, newer construction, and many plain, ranch-style houses on my way down the curved street leading to Lynne's two-story, newly built palatial home. It even had a turret of sorts on the front of it. This particular street didn't have many trees – certainly none of the grand oaks I had in my neighborhood – but the houses on Lynne's side of the street backed up to water. Some part of the bay, no doubt. I glimpsed a dock out back between two houses. Although Lynne's house sat prominently forward on its lot, I noticed that the parcel was large and a green expanse of well-manicured lawn stretched out behind the main house. A guesthouse and a smaller out-building were partially hidden from view beyond the drive.

I waited for a few minutes in my car. I was early and since I didn't know the hostess, I wanted to wait until Weed Lady showed up. I had declined an invitation to ride with Grace. I wanted to appear independent. A few moments after I had parked near Lynne's home, Grace drove up with Twin Vans. *Ugh*.

Frances, I noted, was wearing an Easter get-up. Her brightly colored sweater had several Easter eggs embroidered on it, along with sequins and beads. Her skirt was long with woven ribbons sewed on here and there. *A little plastic Easter grass coming out of her butt and she'd look exactly like an Easter basket.* I chuckled to myself and smoothed my own outfit as I climbed out of the van. For this first meeting, I'd dressed in an understated manner with slacks and a black knit twin-set.

"Hello Grace. Hi Frances," I greeted them on the walkway to the front door. "What's with the orange ribbon, Frances? Support group for those with jaundice?" Twin Vans was sporting a large loop of orange ribbon on her sweater.

"If you watched the news, you'd know we're at an orange level of alert. This is my little way of supporting homeland defense."

Grace shook her head with a wink, discouraging me from further commentary. For her part, Grace was wearing a smooth dress and stylish shoes. They made a small clicking sound on the marble steps.

Lynne greeted us at the door and Grace made the introductions. Lynne led the three of us down a large hallway to what could only be described as a sitting room. We had already passed a formal living room and I could see the French doors down the hall that led to the playroom where a man in a suit (Lynne's husband?) played on a couch with two small children.

The sitting room was a collection of antique chairs and settees that formed a natural conversation area for ten or so people. Nine women were attending the book club meeting tonight. Candles lit about the room softened the light from the three antique lamps dispersed in the corners. A low table in front of a couch held a selection of appetizers and a vase full of delicate flowers. On a buffet along the north wall, silver dish-covers glinted in the flickering light, hiding the treats that awaited us for dinner. Real linen napkins were fanned out next to a selection of silver eating utensils and Royal Doulton china. Crystal wine glasses sat next to some red wine that had already been decanted at some earlier point in the evening.

Someday, I'll be living like this, I thought to myself as my eyes cast about the room taking in all its beauty, right down to the collection of miniature oil paintings, the Italian tile floor, and the Persian rug. The fruit platter on the side table looked like something out of a seventeenth century painting. When Twin Vans waltzed over and plucked one of the fake-looking grapes and popped it into her mouth, I finally broke from my reverie.

The rest of the women were chatting with each other and soon began helping themselves to the wine and the appetizers. I noticed that they were all very well dressed and sporting expensive shoes and accessories. I wished that I had dressed up a little more for the occasion. I followed Grace around for a few minutes to meet everyone and soon we were all sitting with small plates balanced on our laps. The various conversations melded into one about the necessity of taking your dog to a professional groomer. After all, who had time to bathe a dog? Even Grace, who I felt pretty sure was dogless, contributed animatedly to the conversation. Frances, who I knew had that little wiener dog, nodded appreciatively at the comments made by the group as she stuffed her cheeks with soft, ripe cheese and crusty bread. I had been slow to find a seat and was stuck on an ottoman tucked in the corner somewhat behind Twin Van's Easter basket rear-end. Mingling was out of the question from that vantage point.

Eventually, the conversation turned to other subjects such as children and husbands and careers, but by eight o'clock, there was still no mention of the book.

Lynne, our host, got up and uncovered the sumptuous dishes hidden under the silver lids. She invited everyone to fill a plate and return to our seats so that we could start the meeting. *Finally*, I thought, although I hadn't had time to read the book. I'd picked up a paperback copy and skimmed over the back cover that day at lunch. I'd also memorized a few of the suggested book-group questions in the back of the book. When everybody had settled again, I tentatively raised my glass and said, "Cheers." A chorus of responses echoed back the sentiment and I bravely issued forth a "happy Ides of March." It was March fifteenth, but apparently this crowd hadn't read Shakespeare.

Or Flaubert.

Feeling bold, I started out in front of Lynne, asking if everybody else had enjoyed the various motifs as much as I had.

Dead silence.

"What motifs did you like, Janice?" one woman asked.

"What's a motif?" laughed another woman to the gal sitting next to her.

I had only memorized questions, not answers. And of course I hadn't read the book, in high school or recently. "Well, uhm, there seemed to be a motif involving, uhm, trees." I made it up, realizing that nobody seemed to have read the book anyway.

Lynne rescued me. "So how many people did read the book?"

I raised my hand, a little. Several others had at least started it and one woman had finished it only that day but many hadn't even found the time to purchase the book, let alone read it. And nobody save me seemed surprised. Even Lynne hadn't read all of it. And they'd all had a month. *With all their domestic help, nannies, after-school programs, and dog washers, these women don't have any time to read?*

"I really liked it," said the woman who had finished it that day. "It was nice to read something that for a change, wasn't from the perspective of an adolescent girl dealing with the death of a family member."

"Oh, I liked that book," said someone else.

"Which one? We've read about six like that."

I noticed that the woman who had enjoyed Madame Bovary looked a little different from everybody else. Her hair was in a ponytail and she didn't wear any detectable trace of make-up. Wire rimmed glasses perched snootily on her nose. The group intellectual? Around the room, others averted their eyes and shrugged their shoulders.

"Couldn't you just picture the clothes? I wonder if there's a movie version?" asked a different woman between sips of wine.

"Good question! We should have rented it tonight," responded Lynne.

"Actually, that reminds me," said Twin Vans, swallowing a large bite. "I have to get home before nine to see that movie on cable about two women who didn't know that they were married to the same man."

"I saw the preview for that. It looks good."

"I just don't want to get home before the kids are in bed. They'd get all riled up and I'd have to start the whole bed routine from scratch. Better to let Bob handle it."

"To husbands who aren't on the road for a change!"

"Here, here!"

And soon thereafter, book club was finished. Dessert had been offered and declined, as was probably normal. Twin Vans practically pulled Grace out the door to get home in time for her show. I walked over to thank Lynne for the evening.

"Oh you're most welcome. I'm glad to have a new face in the group."

"Your home is really beautiful, Lynne," I offered enthusiastically.

"Oh, thanks. It's growing on me. My designer bought everything and I'm sure it's all top quality but you know, I kind of like contemporary furniture."

"Didn't you tell your designer?"

Lynne laughed. "If only that was the way it worked."

I smiled to cover my confusion. "Well, it's pretty. See you next time."

As I went out the front door, I was surprised to run into the woman with the glasses smoking a cigarette.

"Hey, I'm Nancy. Sorry we didn't get to talk more. Did you enjoy book club?"

"I'm Janice. Yes, I did like it . . ." I trailed off, unsure of how to finish my thought.

"God, we finally pick an interesting book and nobody reads it."

"I'm not sure Lynne even read it."

Nancy smirked. "Lynne doesn't read. She just doesn't want to be left out of anything."

"Why'd she pick a classic then?"

"To impress her husband, I'm sure. He's a lot older than her and went to some Ivy school. This is his second family."

"Oh." I felt that I'd already received too much information and wanted to escape.

Nancy continued. "You know, I can tell that you and I would have a lot in common. We should get together for coffee or something. What's your schedule like tomorrow?"

I thought about the ill-fit Nancy made with the group. Not the best person to buddy-up with. "Yes, well, sometime. Not tomorrow though. I have to wash my dog. Hah, hah. See you next time." I trotted down the sidewalk to my car.

As the others all sped off in their expensive cars, I approached mine with an air of disquiet. My van suddenly appeared dirty and scratched. The interior smelled vaguely of sour milk. The home I was so proud of seemed smallish and plain, in spite of the beautiful tree-lined street. When would I get over my covetous desire for the trappings these other women enjoyed?

27. Session Two

Trudy, Sandy, Pat and three new clients sat in a semi-circle in my family room on a bright Friday morning. The living room was being repainted Folly Green from Farrow & Ball. I also had several new appliances for my kitchen on order, including the oven-fridge and dual dishwasher that Grace swore nobody went without these days. I had bought those on a buy-now, pay-no-interest finance plan.

"Let's get started, shall we?" I stood in front of the group wearing basically the same thing as the week before, only in lime green. "First, I'd like to welcome Karen, Gloria, and Constance to our group. I know you all know each other because your husbands work together. Great!"

Trudy, Sandy and Pat regarded Karen, Gloria, and Constance with slightly superior glances. Trudy, Sandy and Pat had done their homework. They were fully "Grottoed" as I liked to say. Lilly Pulitzer's stock was surely going up in value. Karen, Gloria and Constance had on khakis and tee shirts. *Tsk, tsk*.

"So do you all have children?"

Six nods yes.

"Great. Let's cover kids' issues today. You know, kids provide one of your best opportunities to break into social circles. Use them! Hah, hah."

Six blank stares.

"What I mean, is you have to take them places, don't you? Well, for absolutely free you can hang out at International Plaza's playground with your kids and the next thing you know, you're having a conversation with the woman next to you. And a moment after that, you've scheduled a play date for the kids. Two or three play dates and you're on her Christmas card list. Then it's a barbecue with your husbands and kids, a dinner at a nice restaurant, and an invite to a party where you meet her other friends. Who have kids who need play dates. See what I'm saying? It's simple, really."

Six slow smiles and nods.

"Of course, you have to develop some looks and interests in common with the women you hope to meet. We covered clothes shopping last week and I see it paid off. Karen, Constance, and Gloria, I sent you the handouts last week. You should be getting them soon. Anyway, I have good news on that front."

Six looks of anticipation.

"While you should all start out shopping at places I recommend, like the Pink Grotto, once you've got the styles down, it's perfectly acceptable to hunt for bargains at some of the outlet malls around here. Anyway, back to the kids. Here's some really, really good news. While you wouldn't be caught dead at most bargain mega stores, it is perfectly acceptable to buy your kids clothes at Target."

Six looks of disbelief.

"Oh just play clothes, mind you. For around your own back yard. You'd be surprised whom I have run into shopping in the kids' section at Target. Of course, to hit the mall playground, you'll want to shop at Little Precious. By the way, here are some lists of schools and after-school activities that you'll want to check out. You'll definitely want to get going on the swim lessons at Ms. Sophie's Swim Academy. Everybody takes their kids there from now until about July. It's forty-five minutes, twice a week that you get to spend chatting with other South Tampa moms without interruption from your little darlings."

Sandy had a question. "Don't the moms get to watch the kids swim?"

"Oh sure. The kids aren't that distracting though."

Sandy frowned. I didn't get it.

28. Limbo

After going over my notes from that day's session, I headed to bed. The phone beside the bed rang as soon as I put my head down. It was eleven o'clock.

I cleared my throat before saying "hello."

"Janice? Are you awake?"

It was Jeff. Nobody else called that late.

"I am now. What is it?" I hated these calls. I couldn't talk to Jeff without picturing him laughing and locking arms with Weed Lady. Yet Jeff still called me quite regularly. I was beginning to suspect that Jeff just wanted to keep tabs on my activities. Maybe he wanted to catch me at something that he could use to build his own case for custody of Marcy. *Over my dead body*, I thought.

"I just felt like saying howdy. How is Marcy?"

"She's asleep, Jeff."

"Well I should hope so. I just mean, how is she in general? You know she won't talk to anybody on the phone. When I do manage to get her on the phone, she just starts listing the toys she sees around the room. I think maybe the whole phone concept hasn't sunk in yet."

I shrugged down into my pillows. Jeff was in a talky mood. We still hadn't really talked about our relationship, other than the logistics of having two households. He was obviously over his initial tantrum that had led to his moving in the first place. But we never talked about that, either. And I never once inquired about Weed Lady or any other potentially hot-button topics. We just discussed Marcy, the one topic upon which we had little disagreement. With so much swept under the rug, we actually could carry out civil conversations and after my initial angry reaction each time he called, I usually forgot myself and talked to Jeff at length about Marcy.

I looked over at the photo of Jeff and me on my dresser. I hadn't convinced myself to put it away yet. I pictured Jeff in a sterile, completely neutral apartment. Knowing Jeff, he hadn't bothered to hang any pictures. His golf clubs were probably the main visual in the living room, next to his television. I had insisted that he come back and pick up the big screen thing one day when I'd capriciously decided that Marcy and I were watching too much television. I'd kind of regretted that move since then.

"Say Janice, I noticed that you haven't forwarded any of the joint credit card bills lately. Are you paying them?"

"Oh, sure. I just haven't been using them all that much and I know you never do, being a cash up front kind of guy." In reality, I had been scraping together only enough money to pay the minimum balances that were due. The overall debt was piling up fast. But I couldn't very well let Jeff see what I was buying.

"So I guess you haven't heard that I didn't make salesman of the year."

So that's why he was calling. *How on Earth was I supposed to know?* Jeff's failures were not the sort of thing Ol' Mule Slides would broadcast. "Sorry, Jeff." If he insisted on being a used car salesman, why couldn't he at least be good at it? Who got an MBA and then sold cars? *Ugh. Loser. Horrible, affair-having, neighborhood-slut loving loser.* And so my emotions about Jeff's call ran the usual gamut: anxiety, resignation, and disdain.

"Maybe next time," Jeff muttered. "You know, I've been wanting to speak to you about work."

"I am working."

"My work."

I just couldn't bear another lecture about life's priorities. "Sorry, Jeff. Marcy is coughing again. I've got to run. Next time, okay? See you."

I hung up the phone and sighed. Marcy was fast asleep but I felt restless. I got up and checked out the clothes I had ironed and laid out for the next day: one outfit for wearing around home while I cleaned the toilets and other fun stuff like that (my uniform); one outfit for running errands (cute little capris); and an emergency, you've-been-invited-for-dinner-and-drinks outfit complete with strappy shoes and a light wrap. On days that I had to drop off Marcy at school, I usually had an extra outfit picked out for that task, something that suggested that I was off to play tennis. I spent half my time changing clothes. Luckily, tomorrow was Saturday.

29. Bad News For the Trees

I opened the door to Marcy's room and crept inside. Marcy was in her usual sleep position: on her tummy with her nose to the bed rail, arms splayed across her sheet, blankets in a crumble around her feet. She was wearing her red cowgirl pajamas.

I gently shook Marcy awake. It was eight a.m. "Marcy, Marcy," I whispered. "We have a big day today. Madison's birthday party is at nine thirty and you have a play date with Tinsley this afternoon." I didn't love the idea of such a busy day for Marcy but the Tinsley play date had been arranged before the invitation to Madison's party had arrived. I felt obligated to both. *What the hell, Marcy can nap.*

"What day is it, Mommy?"

"Saturday."

"HAPPY SATURDAY!" Marcy sat up and brushed her bright blond hair away from her face. "Look, I'm already sitting." Marcy thought that each day had a meaning that went with its name. She thought it was sunny every Sunday (and this being Florida, it usually was) and windy every Wednesday.

"Great Honey. So, do you think a lot of kids from your class will be at Madison's party?"

Marcy looked blank for a minute. "Well, JT isn't going to come."

"Why not?"

"Last day he wanted to hold hands with Maddy but Maddy wanted to hold hands with John and Cooper and Miss Jenny told everybody to keep your hands to yourself. Can I have some cereal?"

In the kitchen, I found some Cheerios and a banana for Marcy. The party invitation was taped to the fridge amidst Marcy's latest artistic endeavors. Madison's party was going to be held at a gym. I double-checked the time and location. The invitation specified that kids and parents alike should come prepared for some tumbling fun.

"Guess what, Marcy. We're both going to wear leotards to the party. It's at a gym where they teach tumbling and gymnastics and they're going to play games with all the kids at the party and their mommies too. Cool, huh?" I had purchased matching leotards for Marcy and myself at a small store specializing in sports gear for girls. The leotards had a wild leopard print. I thought that they might be turned into Halloween costumes later in the year, so I'd purchased Marcy's in a size larger than normal. When Marcy had eaten, gone to the bathroom and watched a video, she was finally ready to prepare for the party.

I helped Marcy into her leotard. The crotch drooped a little because of the large size but the rest of it fit pretty well over her toddler size tummy and narrow shoulders. Actually, when she bent over, the rounded front sagged open and exposed Marcy's top half to the world, but she was not the slightest bit self-conscious about it. My leotard fit perfectly. I was still dieting so I'd lost a few pounds and was happily a size ten without sucking in my gut. I had neglected to get tights to match so we both wore thick socks and sneakers and I added pair of stretchy gym shorts over my leotard.

The gym was on Kennedy, a short distance from our house. It gave Marcy just enough time to ascertain from me that one; there would not be strangers at the party, and two; I would stay and be watching the whole time. Marcy's latest worry kick was about strangers. I had made the mistake of telling Marcy not to talk to strangers and that had led to a host of inquiries on the topic. Could mommies talk to strangers? Could daddies? Did strangers talk to other strangers? Just how many strangers were there? There must be a lot of strangers in California.

We arrived slightly late to the party, at nine forty-five, so that we wouldn't be the first to arrive. We found the party in full swing. The moms were all standing around the edges of the room in little groups of three or four, holding cups of coffee and chatting loudly. The kids were all circled up in the middle of the mats listening to the instructions to some game.

Not one child or adult had on gym clothes, let alone jungle print leotards.

Slight panic overtook me as I tried to pull Marcy back out the door. If we ran home quickly, we could change and return to the party by ten, or shortly thereafter. But Marcy squealed loudly at Madison, who was wearing a cardboard crown. "Look, Maddy is a princess. I think she's Snow White and I forgot to bring the dwarf changer." Marcy jumped up and down and cried, nervous about the party and upset that she hadn't brought her pretend dwarf changer (an empty toilet paper roll) so that she could be a dwarf (Bashful, maybe?) to Madison's Snow White. All eyes looked our way.

I sucked it up and put on an air of confidence that quickly crumbled as I was greeted by Madison's mom. Maddy's mom was all gracious and complimentary about our outfits but she was decked out in head-to-toe whatever, complete with alligator slides and a slick new haircut. The moms all looked as if they were participating in a fashion show. They were wearing skirts, slacks, and casual dresses that draped loosely over their size zero bodies. And of course the room was surrounded with floor to ceiling mirrors. Wherever I looked, I saw the reflection of a pot-bellied leopard with chalky white skin, too much lipstick, and an ungraceful ponytail.

"Go and say happy birthday to Madison, Marcy. And look, there are a lot of kids from your class here. No strangers at all. You can pretend you are a dwarf wearing a leopard costume if you want."

"Bah! I'm not Marcy; I'm Grumpy. Hmmph!" Marcy had recovered and was marching out to the circle where she Bah'ed and Hmmph'ed at all the other children who regarded her with trepidation. *There goes the most popular girl in her class.* But I needn't have worried. In no time, all the kids were dwarfs and were marching like little mutineers around an exasperated gym staff member. I faced the other moms, who were all back to their chats, and decided to steel myself with some caffeine.

I found a cup of coffee in a back room where an assortment of bagels, croissants, and fruit beckoned. One other mom was in the room trying to get her two year old to eat some peaches. It wasn't a mom I recognized, probably a friend from the neighborhood or something, not Marcy and Madison's school. The first thing I noticed about her as she crouched by her child, was that she was about my size, that is to say, fairly normal looking. Even so, she was squeezed into the tightest pants I had seen in a long while and her scuffed feet were jammed into tiny little heels that looked brand new and mighty uncomfortable. Her lower back was exposed, thanks to the crouch, and I could see from the tag sticking up that her pants were size two. Pathetic, really, but I felt some sympathy for this woman who obviously felt that it was more important to pass herself off as size two than to be comfortable.

But who was I to be critical? What's worse, pants that ride up your crotch or a slutty looking leotard? *Six of one, half dozen of the other.*

I murmured a hello and left the back room with my coffee. I knew the kids from Marcy's class but not the moms. The girls especially had interesting first names that could be strung together and sound like a made-for-television law firm: Madison, Tinsley, Cooper and Grey. That's right, a girl named Grey. Not to mention the slew of McSomethings. Younger siblings drooled and tottered around the edges of the mats while the party kids whooped it up on the various pieces of equipment that the staff had dragged out. I helped Marcy climb up a few ladders. Marcy had dropped the Grumpy impression at some point. She had a great time and only cried once when a very assertive young girl told her to get off the trampoline.

I avoided conversation with the moms and stuck with the kids, who didn't seem to mind my get-up. When we all assembled in the back room for food and cake, I sat next to Marcy on a kid's chair and dug into some cake while the other moms nibbled on fruit and demurely passed on any kind of confection. So long as I avoided direct eye contact with any adults who weren't wearing a bright purple gym shirt (i.e., the employees), I felt as comfortable as could be expected. The party ended with all the kids taking home a parting gift.

These days, birthday kids don't open their gifts at the party. The gifts sit on display with wrap jobs that easily cost more than the gifts inside. I had actually gone to the South Tampa store where "everyone" went to buy bows. Ten bucks for a pretty bow. I had been stunned but hadn't hesitated to fork over the cash. The store had bows, gifts, and some art prints. It also carried a line of bath accessories that smelled up the back end of the store enough to make me sneeze. *Who bought this stuff?* It was an odd collection and I had quickly arrived at the conclusion that the store stayed in business precisely because all of the proprietor's friends came to the store and paid ten bucks for bows. *Must be some mark-up.* Of course, the bows didn't get put onto wrapped gifts. Nobody wrapped gifts anymore, either. They bagged them. And attached a nice bow.

Gift in hand, I squired a cake-faced Marcy out to the car where Marcy grabbed the tissue-wrapped prize out of its bag. Inside was a porcelain collector's doll in a birthday costume. *Christ!* This little parting gift cost more than the gift Marcy had given the birthday girl. I had a mad notion to run back in and snatch up the gift we'd given Madison to replace it later with something more expensive. But desire to get out of my leopard leotard won in the end and we headed for home. A message awaited us on our answering machine.

"Hi Janice. This is Gretta, Tinsley's mommy. I'm sorry to have to do this but I've got to cancel the play date for this afternoon. How about next week? Tinsley's got a cold."

I deleted the message and called for Marcy. "Sorry Honey, I have some bad news." *Hadn't Tinsley been at the party?*

"Oh, I wish it was good news."

"I know, Sweetie. Tinsley has a cold so we can't play with her today after all."

Marcy contemplated this bit of news. "Mommy? I have some bad news too."

"You do?"

"Yes, today my favorite color is not the same as the trees."

"You mean your favorite color is not green today?"

"Yes. It's pink."

"Well Honey, that is very interesting but it's not really bad news."

"It's bad news for the trees."

I hugged Marcy tight and tried to let Marcy's childish self-confidence rub off on me, right through the leopard print leotard.

30. Saturday Night Grace

Marcy went to bed at around seven o'clock Saturday night. In lieu of the canceled play date, I had taken Marcy and my mom to the zoo. On a beautiful, almost-Spring Saturday afternoon, the zoo was typically crowded. Today had been no exception. The parking lot was a sea of mini-vans and SUVs; gas guzzlin', air pollutin', too-big-for-the-parking-spot cars. And everybody was there to celebrate nature by looking at animals in happy little habitats. The zoo was wonderful. We zoo patrons were a little suspect. We were a little less ecologically minded than we cared to admit. But then, I always had big car guilt until I remembered that it just couldn't be safe for Marcy and me to ride around in a sedan with all these behemoths on the road.

Marcy had been thoroughly worn out at the end of the day and crashed easily once into her pajamas. Marjorie had begged off to read a book and burn some smelly incense in her room. I was contemplating putting on my own pajamas when the phone rang.

I jumped at the sudden noise and wished for once that I'd elected to have caller identification service on my phone. *Incoming outside call.* Who was it? It wasn't very late so it could be anybody. Every possibility made me flinch. *Mule Slides?* She hadn't seen

Marcy this week. *Jeff?* Most likely although shouldn't the Weed Whacker be out on a date with her Graceness? *Mr. Storm?* Thumpa, thumpa, thumpa. I found that possibility a little too frightening.

"Hello?" I said too tersely into the phone.

"I saw your lights were on. Is Marcy in bed? I was wondering if you would like some company? I've got a bottle of red if you've got a remote control. Hee, hee."

Grace? So no date tonight, eh Honey-pot? Jeff was probably parked at some fast food parking lot along with a hundred other car geeks fawning over paint jobs and hood ornaments. Grace rose slightly in my estimation, given that she'd elected not to go. Maybe Grace was already discovering what a bore Jeff could be at times.

"Uhm, sure. Come on over. Marcy's asleep. I was going to watch *Trading Spaces*, you know, that show where they make over neighbor's rooms?"

"I love that show! I'll be right over. Get out a wine glass. Mine is already poured."

Lush.

Grace arrived just as I was finishing a hurried sweep of the downstairs bathroom. "Coming!" I yelled as Grace knocked lightly on the front door. "Hi Grace. This is a surprise."

"I know. I hope it's okay. I get tired of sitting around on Saturday nights sometimes." Giggle, giggle, nose scrunch.

Jeff must be doing the car thing a lot. Or maybe he's already stepping out with yet another woman. Interesting thought. "Well, I happen to be home tonight too so we might as well have a drink. Let me get the phone and we'll sit in the living room. I'm expecting a call." *Lie.*

"Oh, I love the color, Janice. Has it changed? It looks different, anyway."

"Nope. Same color. Have a seat." *Lie number two. Better stop counting.*

Grace poured us both a glass of wine. I could see that Grace had already been dipping into the bottle. I got up briefly to fetch another bottle of red from the pantry. A drunk Grace might be a chatty Grace, although the giggle level might become unbearable.

Grace sighed and slid off her shoes. She settled back into the red couch and draped her arms over the back. "So, Janice, what do you make of our little neighborhood?"

"Oh, well, it's great. I mean I was familiar with it before we moved in. Jeff's mother lives nearby."

"How is that working?"

"Fine," I said guardedly.

"Good. I could never live in the same *state* as my mother-in-law."

"You're married?"

"Past tense. Divorced five years ago. My ex was a downer. Too pessimistic. Life's too short not to be happy, you know?"

"Sure. So, no kids?"

"Nada. But I'm thinking of borrowing some."

I smiled in spite of myself. "Whatever for? I mean I love Marcy more than life itself but if I was single . . ." I trailed off. *Am I single?*

"If you haven't noticed, the only way to get an in around here is to have a husband who makes a lot of money so you can stay home and join Junior League, and have kids you can dress up and press into friendships with the other kids of the people you want to impress." Grace guzzled her wine and got a refill, apparently not expecting a response from me.

"I assume you work?" I asked.

"I'm an attorney. Solo practitioner."

"What kind of cases do you handle?" *Clowns? Just not divorce, please not divorce.* Jeff was a bore but he was still my bore, legally anyway. I wasn't quite ready to give that up. A notion that surprised me.

"Real estate. Pretty boring. Do you work?"

I thought hard about my answer. This could be getting back to Jeff. "Yes. I'm a consultant."

"What kind?"

"Oh, business stuff, you know. Shall I open the new bottle?"

"Absolutely!" Giggle.

We sipped in silence for a few minutes until I got up and put on some jazz.

"Stanley Jordan? I have this CD."

I was having an internal struggle. I was finding that I liked Grace a little. She reminded me of the friends I'd had before I got married. Carefree but sophisticated. Fun. "It's great, isn't it?"

Grace nodded agreement. "I played this very same CD for our neighbor across the street and she thought it was too 'out there.' What does that mean? Sure it's not prepackaged, jazz light hits, but come on, Stanley Jordan? He's not exactly, well, out there."

"Are you talking about Twin Vans?"

"Who? Oh, that's funny. Who the hell buys two of the same van, anyway? Hee, hee."

"It doesn't show much imagination. I'll bet she schedules sex with her husband while she's planning the weekly meals on her calendar." *Wow, the wine is kicking in.*

Grace laughed. "And I'll bet she closes her eyes."

"I would if I were married to her husband."

More laughing. We chatted for a while longer until we were out of wine and easy topics for conversation.

"I better get going. Thanks for letting me crash in on you. Whew, glad I'm walking." Grace looked a little unsteady.

"Anytime, Grace. I'll see you around. Oh, and thanks again for inviting me to join your book club. It was fun."

"Sure. Sorry you didn't have a chance to read the book." Grace winked at me and headed out the front door.

How'd she know?

31. Wishes

On Sunday morning, I got my wish. Gregory Storm called and invited Marcy and me over for a barbecue that afternoon. A romantic dinner date couldn't be far off.

"We'd love to come. What can I bring?"

"Why don't you bring a bottle of your favorite wine? I've got everything the kids will want. Come over around four."

"See you then!"

Of course, Jeff called immediately after I'd replaced the phone in its cradle.

"Is Marcy ready?"

"Ready for what?" I was perplexed.

"I told you last week it was Mom's birthday today. I'm taking Marcy over for cake."

"God, Jeff, I completely forgot. Can we make it another day instead?"

"You want Mom to reschedule her birthday?"

"No, I mean . . . oh hell, what time is the party?"

"Two o'clock."

"Fine. But you have to have Marcy back before four o'clock. We've got some other plans."

"No problem."

Maybe this would work out all right. I could go grab a bottle of wine while Jeff had Marcy over at Mule Slides. *Now, what to wear.* Oh, and Marcy needed a gift for her grandmother. That should be Jeff's problem but he wouldn't think of it and it was still in Marcy's and my best interest to keep the old lady happy.

Marcy was downstairs watching television.

"Hi Honey. Want to make a present for Granny? It's her birthday today."

"Yes, yes. Can I glue?"

"Sure thing." I settled Marcy down at the kitchen table with a bottle of glue, some colored markers, and a few empty toilet paper rolls. "Go for it, Sweetie."

Later, after Jeff had picked up Marcy and a freshly minted, super deluxe Grandma-size dwarf changer, I got into full throttle with respect to the afternoon's date at the Storms. I tried on several pairs of pants and settled on some denim style cropped pants with a striped tee shirt. My hair looked pretty good already so I didn't change that. I pondered the longest over what shoes to wear. I wanted to wear my little slip-on canvas sneakers because they suggested a nautical theme and I craved an invite on the yacht. But they were awfully casual. Better to stick with something leather.

I dashed out to the wine store that had just opened. For some stupid reason, you couldn't buy alcohol in any form before one o'clock on Sundays in this town. Maybe all of Florida, who knew? And for what reason? All those Sunday morning tipplers surely knew to stock up on Saturday night. They probably weren't going to go to church anyway and even if everybody in the whole state went to Sunday morning services, why shouldn't they be able to stop at the grocery store on the way home to buy a six-pack to drink while they watched sports in the afternoon? No harm, no foul, as Jeff would say. *Ugh, no fond Jeff thoughts today.*

When I got home at three thirty, Jeff and Marcy were already there, playing in the front yard. Marcy's dress was covered with ice cream and cake crumbs. Jeff had on jeans and a golf shirt. *Of course.*

"Hi guys. Thanks, Jeff. Marcy, why don't you go inside and use the potty? We've got to get going."

"Where are you guys headed?" Jeff asked.

"Marcy has a play date this afternoon."

"Oh? She didn't mention it. Who with?"

"She didn't mention it because she doesn't know about it yet. You know how she gets. How much cake did she eat?"

"Oh, a lot more than you'd probably let her."

"Jeff, what the hell does that mean?"

"Don't start, Janice. I was just making a joke. How are you doing, anyway? Maybe we should get together soon and talk. Like grown-ups, you know, without yelling, about some real issues, stuff like that."

I had a panicky feeling that Jeff wanted to discuss divorce. How did I feel about that? Better to put it off. I wasn't ready for the floor to drop out from under me just yet. I didn't have a replacement lined up. *Did I want a replacement? I sure as hell didn't want to be alone.*

"Yeah, sure, but I'm pretty busy lately. I'm doing great, by the way. Never better. Well, I gotta run. You have my number." I abruptly headed towards the front door. I felt an urgent desire to cry.

"I miss you Janice."

The words stung as much as they helped. I missed him too. So I made light. "Of course you do. I'm very desirable, you know." I laughed and went into the house, my emotions knotted into a tight ball. "Come on Marce, let's go."

32. Twang Went the Strings of My Heart

The Storms lived in a large house in Old Hyde Park. A banner on the front marked the house as a registered historic landmark. All the houses on the street were large, well kept, and vaguely imposing. In spite of the neighborhood's proximity to some less desirable real estate a few blocks over, one got the feeling that in this neighborhood, you wouldn't find the usual riff-raff slouching around on the sidewalks. Everything was too tidy. Nobody even bothered with curtains. You could see right into the front rooms of most of the homes.

Gregory's house had a large front yard and a narrow driveway. As Marcy and I got out of our car, I could smell the scent of food on the grill. I decided that we should just head to the back yard. We found all three Storm boys tossing around a football on the grass. They looked like an advertisement for Ralph Lauren.

"Hello boys. Do you allow girls to play?"

I pried Marcy off of my pants leg and shoved her towards the ball game.

"Go say hi to Lucas, Honey."

Lucas waved at Marcy and heaved the small football in her direction. *How did he learn to throw like that?* The spiraling ball struck Marcy full in the face. Marcy hadn't even thought to lift her hands up and knock it away, let alone catch the ball. Blood spurted out of her nose, adding a nice red tint to the front of her already party-smeared dress.

Gregory immediately took charge. He sent Jack to get some ice and grabbed a bar towel from the table to press onto Marcy's face. Mercifully, Marcy wasn't screaming at the top of her lungs. Not yet, anyway. She was still in shock or something. They had her lean forward while I gently pinched her nostrils together. The bleeding stopped within a few minutes and Marcy surprised everybody with a smile.

"I sprang a leak, Mommy."

"You surely did, Sweetie. But I think we've plugged it up for now. Do you want to lie down or anything?"

"Can I swing?"

"Of course!" Gregory and I marveled over Marcy's resilience as she and Lucas headed for the deluxe swing set. Jack returned with some ice in a plastic bag.

"I'll take that son." Gregory grabbed the ice and tipped it into two glasses. "How about some lemonade?"

"Thanks. That reminds me, here's the wine. It's red because I assumed you guys would be grilling up steaks. If it's fish or chicken, red is still the best choice, in my opinion."

"We're vegetarians," Gregory stated without a hint of sarcasm, or condemnation.

I glanced at Gregory's face and the grill and then the children, hoping for some indication as to whether or not he was joking. "Well, nothing better than a full-bodied red with a Portobello steak." *Smooth, sister.*

I still didn't know if Gregory had been kidding until he served us all stir-fry with tofu and green beans. Luckily, he also had cooked up a couple of veggie hot dogs or Marcy would surely have let him know that the only proper use for a green bean is to poke it up your nose.

The sky darkened as we ate at the outdoor table. The built-in gas grill/outdoor kitchen was turned off and a Mexican looking outdoor fireplace was turned on. The glow from the fire and the light from the tiki torches softened the atmosphere, creating the perfect ambiance for the red wine and the sleepy kids.

"If you'd like to stay a while, I could get a bed ready for Marcy to lie down on. She looks pretty beat."

"Well, we do have this wine to finish."

"Let's move inside. Come on boys. Go get bathed and let me see how well you can brush your teeth."

I scooped up a dirty, tired Marcy and felt guilty that I wasn't running her right home for her own bath and bed. As I went inside, I admired the antiques in the hallway and noticed the coziness of the family room. A gas fire insert in the fireplace stood ready to light up at a moment's notice with the push of a button. Toys had been put away and a stereo already played soft music. What was that? Country music? *Yikes.*

I heard Gregory upstairs with the boys and made the grown-up decision to take Marcy home. As tempting as another glass of wine felt, parental duty was overwhelming my desire to flirt. Marcy looked like a wreck and didn't appear to want to let go of my neck. Besides, she was wearing a vaguely familiar blanched expression.

Gregory came downstairs. "I've got the guest bed ready for Marcy."

"I'm so sorry, Gregory. Thanks for everything. We've had a lovely time but Marcy is spent. I'll take a rain check on that wine." I glanced at Marcy's face and rushed out the front door so Marcy could puke all over the spring annuals that had been planted near the front walkway. I wiped at Marcy's mouth with my shirt and kicked dirt up at the soiled flowers. Gregory stepped outside with my purse and regarded us with some amusement.

"I think you'll need your car keys."

"I am so sorry. I'm really embarrassed." I immediately regretted my words. I didn't want Marcy to feel responsible. "How about I talk to you later. I need to get my little sweetie home."

"Take care." Gregory Storm backed into his house and shut the door. Marcy had a couple more dry heaves as we made our way to the car.

It seemed that Marcy's throwing up was punctuating a lot of important moments in my life. *Was there a cosmic message that I was missing?*

33. Session Three

"So ladies, shall we talk about fitness?" I had dropped another two pounds since the weekend, thanks to a diet of dry cereal, vitamins, and red wine. Since the birthday party drama at the gym, I'd been considering a naked truth that heretofore I'd been underestimating. Skinny women have more clout. And, this was the really good part, losing weight is cheap. Free, actually.

The collection of women in my living room possessed the usual variety of shapes and sizes. Poor Constance couldn't be more than five feet tall and that didn't leave a lot of frame to carry all those pounds. Trudy was tall and thin and had that ravishing red hair. But everybody else was more or less like me. Normalish.

"I don't mean to suggest that you all don't look great. Nice clothes, by the way. Pink Grotto's employees must be enjoying their commissions. But is there any woman alive who wouldn't feel just a little bit happier, if not downright ecstatic to buy the same outfit in a size or two smaller? I know I would and I'm working on it."

"What are you doing? Weight Watchers? Jenny Craig?"

"I'll get to that. Just close your eyes and picture your last big full-dress party. Maybe it was the holiday party for your husband's firm or some fundraiser. Put yourself there and picture two women talking to each other. One is holding a small glass of wine . . ." I pictured the Fruit Ball.

"Red or white?" Chuckles.

"Doesn't matter. Anyway, the other is holding a plate of appetizers and while she talks, she's chewing up a big bite of some cheesy concoction. Maybe she even has a drip of oil on her chin." I paused for effect. "Got it? Now, which one is better dressed?"

Several smiles wandered across the faces of the women in the room. They got it. I didn't wait for a response.

"I'll bet that for every one of you, the woman with the wine is sophisticated, impeccably dressed, and THIN! I'll bet the minute I mentioned the plate of food and the sweets, you pictured a dowdy woman with a bright dress. I'll bet that if I told you that one of those two women was going to walk over to you and let you in on a little secret, you'd hope for the thin one. Who wouldn't want to be in her confidence?"

Heads nodded slightly as eyes opened up. Everybody looked at the tray of food I had laid but nobody grabbed a doughnut.

"Cruel, I know." I picked up the tray and whisked it back into the kitchen. When I returned, the other women were sipping their coffees and discussing various diets.

I took charge again. "I know I began this session a couple of weeks ago talking about clothes and we will be discussing clothing and accessories several more times before this is all over. But wouldn't you all have to agree that one edge a thin woman has over the rest of us is the ability to wear pretty much anything and look great? Especially if she has a good haircut."

Somebody asked, "How does it feel, Trudy?" Yuk, yuk.

"Okay, not everybody in this group needs to work on weight. But I have to speak in generalities, now don't I? And even Trudy might benefit from being reminded about the general principle that you don't eat at parties. Stay focused on your image, ladies. Anyway, the really great news is that while you are all moving down to South Tampa to smaller houses with double the mortgage, paying moving costs, probably sticking your kids into private schools, etc., losing weight is a low cost proposition. Not that it's not worth the move, you know. To South Tampa I mean. Well, you know what I mean. Anyway, losing weight is cheap." I halted the spew of words.

"That's true."

"I guess it is. I never thought about it that way."

"Can't we do a diet program?"

I quieted the chatter. "Can I just remind everybody that I am not a medical professional? You'll all have to figure out the best way yourselves. I just want to get you to focus on the importance of this particular goal."

"Thanks!"

I sat down and stirred my coffee. I'd just told six women to go on a diet and they were thanking me. Paying me. *Life is good.*

The rest of the meeting was spent discussing weight-loss tactics. One of the clients asked me an interesting question.

"What about exercise?"

I smiled. "That's for next time. Actually, the specific topic is memberships in clubs, including athletic clubs. I guess it doesn't really matter if you actually exercise or not, does it? It's the belonging that counts. See you next week."

34. Wishes Can Come True

Our first real date was set for Saturday night. Gregory had found me at school drop-off and asked me to dinner. I had been so flustered I'd accepted and run away without inquiring about where we were going to eat. Now it was Saturday morning and I had to figure out what to wear. Margaret was going to come over with the boys to watch Marcy. I felt bad about asking her to do it but I couldn't very well ask Jeff or his mother to baby-sit while I went on a date. Marjorie had "plans" and Kate had practically moved into Gus's house.

I played the closet game again. Nothing was quite right. I wanted to be both casual and elegant, without being overdressed or costumed up. At the same time, I didn't want to be *too* casual, like someone who wouldn't be expecting to be taken to a fine restaurant. I picked up the phone and called Margaret.

"Is it better to be over-dressed or under-dressed?"

"In my experience, the true southern woman fears being over-dressed more than being under-dressed. Of course the kicker is that the true southern woman is already better dressed on a casual Saturday than your average Yankee in her work clothes."

"Margaret, I'm from New York."

"Right. But you live in Florida now, Honey. This Gregory Storm sounds like something of a southern gentleman to me. Better put yourself in southern frame of mind."

"But he's a vegetarian."

"A *southern* vegetarian."

"Thanks. Gotta run."

I picked out a silk knit sweater and a matching skirt. I finished the outfit with brand new, rather high-heeled black boots. It was the kind of outfit that could work just about anywhere, I decided. Besides, the boots made me feel like a dominatrix. Who wouldn't feel confident dressed in these boots? They'd cost a fortune but I had a store credit card. Saks. I had a Saks card. *Did life get any better than that?*

Once my outfit was established, I found that I had an even harder time picking underclothes. If I stuck with my comfortable, all cotton high-cut briefs, I would be comfortable all night and there would be no way on Earth I could be talked out of my clothes. My granny pants were for my eyes only. And Jeff's for the past few years but that didn't count. So, that begged the question, did I wish to be talked out of my clothes?

A small shiver of excitement slipped up my spine as I thought about kissing the oh-so-handsome Gregory Storm. Excitement turned to nervous sweat when I considered those strong masculine hands wandering up under my sweater. It had been forever since anybody but Jeff had groped me. Maybe college. That's probably why I remembered it as groping rather than something gentle and sweet, say, caressing. *Too much angst. Granny pants it is.*

Later, when Margaret arrived with the boys, I realized how long it had been since I'd actually seen Margaret. "Have you lost weight, Margaret?"

"Twenty pounds, more or less. Depends on the time of the month and whether or not I'm bloated like a dead cow."

"You look amazing!"

"You look pretty trim yourself. Nice boots, Lady. I wish we wore the same size."

I regarded Margaret for a minute. Margaret was slimmer, her hair was coiffed, and her clothes were practically hip. "Are you seeing somebody, Margaret?"

Margaret gave me the arched-eyebrow look and said, "Isn't it obvious?"

I stared at Margaret mindful of the long pause and loud heart palpitations. "Well . . .?"

"I met a guy at work."

I exhaled with a too-loud laugh. "Margaret Oaks, how many times have you pinky-sworn that you would not date your boss?"

"Who said it was my boss? His name is Gary and he's a clerk in the men's department. Get this, he's fifteen years my junior." Margaret gave me a defiant smile. "And he is fit as a fiddle."

"What does that mean, anyway?" I was smiling but inside my emotions were mixed.

"Ready to be played? How the hell should I know? The point is that Gary is way into weight lifting. And me, I might add."

"Hmmm, great." I tried to remain enthusiastic but the truth was that I felt that Margaret was dating somebody I would have rejected clear back in college for lack of ambition. Wasn't Margaret considering her kids? What did some young stud have to offer her, besides a good excuse not to wear Granny pants? The realization made me inexplicably uncomfortable. *What kind of prude am I becoming?*

Marcy and the boys ran into the front hallway where Margaret and I were standing. "Mommy, Cory and Cameron said that if I didn't let them take Barbie's head off, they were going to make me dead. What's dead, Mommy?"

Now? She had to ask such an important question right *now*? Gregory's Mercedes was pulling into the driveway. "Marcy, Honey, you don't have to let the boys take Barbie's head off. And they won't kill you, I promise. Why don't you let Miss Margaret get you a box of juice and she'll explain what dead means for you."

"Me?" Margaret looked alarmed.

"It was your kids who taught her the word. You all can figure out an explanation for her. I don't think I'll be all that late. Wish me luck!"

"Luck!!"

35. Be Careful What You Wish For

As I walked outside to greet Gregory, I felt another shiver. It was a delightful evening, warm enough to dine outside. Maybe he was going to take me over to the beach to eat on some terrace overlooking the water. Or maybe we would do something even more upscale, like have a drink at a nice hotel lounge and dine on the top floor overlooking the city. After all, I had reason to believe that Gregory enjoyed a fine meal and that money was not a problem.

"Hi Gregory," I greeted him as he scooted around his car to open the door on my side. *Ah, a gentleman for sure.*

Gregory gave me a light peck on the cheek. "I'm so glad we could get together tonight."

"Where are the boys?" I regretted that line of banter immediately. They were obviously with the former Mrs. Storm and I didn't want Gregory thinking about her tonight.

"They're at a sleep over. Here you go."

I climbed into the car. The radio was playing very loudly. Country music twanged out of the speakers. Real, old-fashioned country, not even crossover country-light. I quickly turned down the volume as Gregory made his way back to his side of the car and got in.

"This is a nice car. Have you had it long?" I silently thanked Jeff for his car obsession. At least I could discuss automobiles with some authority. I wondered briefly where Jeff was tonight. I glanced at Grace's windows as we passed her house. All dark.

"I've had this car for about a year." He seemed dismissive of the topic. "I lease a new car every couple of years so I never have to worry about upkeep. I'm not too handy when it comes to working on cars and I don't have time to be dropping it off somewhere all the time."

Jeff can fix anything with wheels. Stop it!

"So where are we going tonight?" I had already planned out what I would order to seem sophisticated and concerned for my health. A small salad with dressing on the side, grilled fish, some red wine.

"I thought I would take you to my favorite place. You look like a gal who can eat a steak." He smiled and headed out for the Interstate.

What the hell does it mean that I look like I can eat a steak? Where the hell are we going? Didn't he say that he was a vegetarian?

He drove us up to Carrollwood, exactly a mile from where I used to live. I may as well have dropped Marcy off at Margaret's instead of the other way around. I felt a little gloomy that the only people who were going to see me out with Gregory Storm were the unimpressionable folks from my old hood. All the restaurants on this stretch of Dale Mabry were chains, except for . . ..

"Here we are!" Gregory was all smiles as he pulled into the parking lot of The Lasso, a steakhouse and line-dancing club featuring, *choke*, an all you can eat buffet.

I folded down the window shade to check myself in the mirror. I knew my makeup looked fine, I just needed to check the expression on my face. I twisted my mouth into a quirky smile and put on my best game face. *After all, this could be fun. Right?*

We went inside where the hostess, who looked all of twelve, knew Gregory by name and flirted with him effortlessly as she showed us to a table near the dance floor.

"Do you line dance?" Gregory asked.

"Not since my girlfriend's bachelorette party a few years ago." I glanced apprehensively at the dance floor where a couple of women were tripping their way through some steps being demonstrated by a cute young man in a large hat.

"It's early yet. The dance floor really heats up a little bit later. Ah, there you are." A waitress had approached the table and asked for a drink order. "I'll have the Lasso Margarita. Make that two, you just have to try one." He winked at me. "We can go ahead and order dinner now, too."

I hadn't even cracked open my menu.

"Bring the lady the prime rib supper and we'll both do the all-you-can-eat." To me he said, "The all-you-can-eat counter has hot side dishes and a salad bar that's to die for. Come on, I'll show you."

Apparently we weren't even going to wait for our drinks to come. Gregory led me to the buffet table where congealed macaroni and cheese beckoned from between not one, but two flavors of wiggly Jell-O. I became conscious of a nagging squeeze on my big toe from the new boots that made me alarmingly tall next to the shortish Gregory Storm. Why hadn't I noticed his stature before? I would have worn lower heels. I examined the food choices. It was a two-year-old's fantasy. Mac and cheese, Jell-O, cheese toast, potato salad (mostly mayonnaise), crinkle fries, scalloped potatoes, baked potatoes with sour cream and bacon sides, a greenish looking potato entrée that looked alarmingly like curry, and mini-wieners in baked beans. The salad bar was iceberg lettuce, shredded carrots, shredded cheese, shredded hard-boiled eggs, and croutons. No light dressing here, I noticed.

Gregory had charged ahead, piling his plate with all kinds of potato (minus the green dish) and a mound of lettuce. He squirted about a gallon of ranch style dressing onto it and topped it with a handful of cheese. "See you back at the table." He headed away crunching a crouton.

I was paralyzed. I was looking at this food and thinking about Bern's Steakhouse, Tampa's most famous steak restaurant. I'd never eaten there. *If I look so much like the kind of woman who could eat a steak, why the hell didn't he take me to a decent steakhouse?* I chose a couple of greasy french fries and made myself a small salad. I wasn't at all concerned about my image at this point. I just wanted to avoid food poisoning.

Back at our table, Gregory was sucking down the last of his margarita. Already. He gestured to the waitress to bring another round. I sat down and took a sip of my drink. It was good but very strong. Gregory waited for me to put my drink down.

"I told you they were good, didn't I? How's your salad? I can just eat and eat their salad here. Their dressing is so good." He launched into his food, washing down bites with his drink – his second drink in twenty minutes. Before I had taken even one bite of lettuce, Gregory remarked about how glad he was that I wasn't one of those women you take out for a nice dinner and they don't eat a thing. *Super*. Nothing like being told you look like someone who loves to eat to make you have absolutely no interest in that activity whatsoever.

I nibbled at my salad but before I'd made any headway, my steak arrived. I wondered just how fast this meal was going to be over. Maybe not fast enough. My feet hurt. At least my underwear was comfortable. The steak looked juicy and rare enough to moo.

"Eat up and I'll show you a few dances. The music is going to get started soon."

I looked around. There was music playing already but now I saw a band setting up on a stage across the dance floor. Wow, if they used the same cows to get the steak and create all that leather clothing, it was pretty efficient use of the poor beasts. Not that I had any problem eating beef. Cooked would be nice though.

We ate our dinners. I still had both the salad and dinner plates before me, making it awkward to eat neatly. And since I didn't want to examine my food too closely, well, it was inevitable that some of it would drip on my sweater. I dabbed at it with my napkin. Almost immediately the live music began blaring and Gregory grabbed my hand. He pulled me out onto the dance floor where he deftly maneuvered us to the front of the pack.

"Just do what I do," Gregory yelled at me as everybody else around us stomped, clapped, jumped and nearly knocked me over. After a few minutes, I used sign language to let Gregory know that I needed to use the bathroom. He smiled and waved me off. Once I got off the dance floor, I went back over to our table and took a sip of my water and sat down. I unzipped my boots, hoping my toes would feel a little relief but it was no use. I was miserably uncomfortable, dressed completely inappropriately for this jeans-wearing crowd, and slowly going deaf thanks to the volume at which the band was playing. I sat back and tried to locate Gregory on the dance floor.

From what I could tell, line dancing was sort of a single's sport. You didn't need a partner and some of the lines were mostly comprised of women in short fringy skirts. Gregory had moved to the side where a waitress served up drinks on the high railing around the dance floor. Gregory was glugging another margarita. I ordered a cup of coffee from the over-the-top cheerful waitress and decided to feign illness or something to get Gregory to leave this place. It was a good plan, however, Gregory Storm, the lean mean dancing machine, stayed out on the dance floor for at least six or seven more drawn out songs. I lost count of his margaritas. When I did see him, he was stumbling towards our table with a large grin and an empty drink glass.

"Isn't this band great?" he asked as he more or less fell into his chair.

I didn't bother to answer. All the charm, sophistication, and appeal I had read into his persona had apparently been in my head. He was a drunk with bad taste in music and food. Money alone didn't make you worthy and being a vegetarian didn't give you good taste. Something to remember for my consulting group. Now, should I get a cab?

Gregory waved the waitress over to the table. "You want another one?" he asked me before he ordered.

"I think maybe I need to be getting home," I replied, shaking my head "no" to the waitress.

"I like your thinking," Gregory slurred back. He got up, and showing a modicum of responsibility, handed me the car keys. "I guess you better drive." He sauntered out the door after giving me a quick wink. I stood there with the expectant waitress and realized that I was going to have to pay for our dinner.

I found Gregory standing next to the car grinning. His eyes were slung low with alcohol. He tried to nuzzle me as I opened the car door but I shrugged him off. He got inside and leaned his head back. By the time I got into the driver's seat, he was snoring. I got out my phone and called Margaret.

"You just won't believe this evening. Do me a favor, crack open a bottle of red wine for you and me and call a taxi to meet me at Gregory's house. Here's his address. I'll be there in about twenty-five minutes."

"Wow, I can't wait to hear this. I'll get you a cab. Are you okay?"

"Of course. But my date is asleep and I'm driving the car to his house. I imagine he'll still be asleep in the car come morning."

"Too funny. Come on home. You'll have to tell me all about it another time though. Gary is waiting for me back at my place. See you."

I felt the last of the wind going out of my sails. If nothing else, I had to admit that I missed the certainty of Jeff.

36. A Nice, Casual Interview

Monday morning arrived with a surprise. Mule Slides had come through with the school interview at St. X and she told me that Marcy was on the interview wait-list at St. Y. St. Z. wasn't going to happen this year.

"That is so great! I really can't thank you enough. When is the interview?" I inquired.

"One thirty."

Laugh, laugh. "No, I mean what date?"

"Today, dear. One thirty. Go in through the double doors. She'll be meeting with a teacher or two, I imagine."

Today? I nearly passed out. What time was it? Eight o'clock. Okay, hours to get ready. No preschool this morning. A little cram session was in order.

"Well, thanks again, Mrs. Dower." I replaced the phone in the kitchen and found Marcy snuggled up on the couch watching Snow White. Marcy no longer watched the beginning where the jealous queen had Snow White taken to the woods to be killed by the huntsman. And she never watched the housecleaning portion, either. She fast-forwarded directly to the part where the funny little men were mining diamonds and singing with their echoes. Lately, Bashful was her favorite.

Curled up under the blanket, Marcy suddenly looked very small and young. She was only three, after all. She wouldn't be four for a couple of months. How could it be that she was about to have one of the most important interviews of her young life?

"Marcy, can I turn off the television? We need to talk."

"Is it time for preschool? I didn't have my waffle yet. Can I eat it in the car?"

"You don't have regular preschool today, Honey. You and I are going to go check out a school that Daddy used to go to when he was a kid. There's a teacher there that would like to play with you for a few minutes. Won't that be fun?"

Marcy regarded me with cool eyes. "There's no preschool for any kids?"

"Not exactly. You are going to be absent today. Remember how other kids are absent sometimes?"

"Do I have a fever?"

"No, Sweetie. You're fine. You're just going to go visit another school for one day. You'll like it."

"Will my teachers be there?"

"No . . ."

"Will I have a place to put my snack?"

"No, you are not eating snack at the new school."

"I'm not eating snack today?"

"I didn't say that. You'll eat snack at home. Lunch too, just like always. Then we'll go. Why don't I make you that waffle now." I got up before Marcy could ask any more questions or work herself up into a snit. I made myself coffee while the frozen waffle toasted.

Acting casual, I brought the waffle out to Marcy and asked her, in passing, if she knew our address.

"The forest."

"What?" But I knew that Marcy had shifted to dwarf mode. "Marce, it's very important that you be Marcy today. You don't live in the dwarf's house today."

Marcy looked at me intently: "I don't actually live in a castle, either."

It was going to be one of those days.

By one o'clock, I had not successfully coerced one proper response out of Marcy. I had managed to squeeze her into a dress and some fancy black shoes. "Come on. We better go check out that school."

We arrived with time to spare and found ourselves seated in a small foyer waiting for the director of admissions. A very nice looking woman came out to greet us. Before the woman could say anything to her, Marcy began reciting: "I'm Marcy Pintoff. M . A . R . C . Y. I live in Tampa, Florida. My phone number is 555-6871. And, uhm, uhm, oh yeah, 10, 9, 8, 7, 6, 5, 4, 3, 2, 1, ZERO!!" Marcy gave me a Mona Lisa smile.

The admission's director also gave me a smile that I had little difficulty deciphering.

"Perhaps you'd both like to come into my office for a few minutes before Marcy's interview."

I wanted to die. Oh well, at least Marcy had benefited from this morning's coaching in some small regard. She'd never known her phone number before today. Maybe St. Y would come through.

In the woman's office, Marcy spied a family picture. Two parents, two kids, two dogs. Probably two goldfish at home too. "I have a mommy and a daddy."

"That's wonderful, Marcy."

"And even though my daddy doesn't live with me, he still loves me every day."

The woman raised her eyebrows towards me.

"Just a temporary separation." I felt defensive. "Marcy, why don't you tell this nice lady about your favorite color."

"Well, Bashful wears a green hat."

"Is green your favorite color, Marcy? It's mine too."

"And Princess Zoomoo's."

"Princess Zoomoo?" Again with the raised eyebrows.

I interrupted, "It's her name for a mermaid we saw at Weeki Wachee. Marcy, maybe the lady has some questions for you."

"Bashful's favorite food is ice cream. It has his name on it."

Ugh.

"Do you watch a lot of television, Marcy?"

"Oh yes!"

Double ugh. Luckily, Marcy's actual interviewer showed up just then to lead Marcy to another room.

Later, with an assurance that we'd be hearing from the school soon about its admission decision, Marcy and I left St. X. I had no idea what had been discussed between Marcy and the teacher during her interview but judging from the teacher's perplexed expression, I deduced that Marcy had regaled her with stories of dwarf changers and other such nonsense. If she was really lucky, Marcy had spoken to her in the made-up language that she called "French."

"Marcy, Honey?"

"Yes mommy?"

"You know that dwarfs are just make-believe don't you? Snow White is just a story."

"Oh, riiiggghhht," Marcy responded with a perfect drawn-out Mommy impression.

37. Session Four

On Wednesday, I struggled a bit to put together an outfit for the group meeting. I didn't have the resources to buy too many new clothes all at once. Maybe if I wore the sleeveless cable knit with the green pants, nobody would notice that I was recycling. Marcy was already at school. She'd been eager to get to school that morning because I had told her that we would be celebrating her birthday soon and that she would get to have a party. Marcy's birthday wasn't until May but I was anxious for an excuse to host something. I was planning an April party, maybe at the park.

By the time Trudy arrived first, I had myself pulled together, at least physically. I had promised the group that we would discuss memberships today and on that topic I was shaky at best. I still didn't really belong to anything. Except Grace's book club. At least that was something.

"Hi Trudy. Come in. I got us some low-fat muffins from The Bakery. Help yourself."

The rest of the group arrived shortly thereafter and I got started. Adrenaline would carry me through. That, and a lot of caffeine. Of course my mother sauntered in about then.

"Oh, everyone, this is my mother, Marjorie. Did you need something, Mother?" I gave my mom a pointed look.

"I just wanted to listen in. You ladies don't mind, do you?"

I let everybody assure Marjorie that she was welcome before launching into my discussion. Why did my mom have to watch today? I wasn't feeling on top of my game and I certainly didn't need an audience. Especially my mother in some gauzy turquoise Indian garment she'd taken a fancy to at a thrift shop.

"Okay, ladies. Oh Constance, that is a great shirt. Where did you find it?"

"My sister sent it to me from New York."

"Hummm . . ."

"What?" Constance looked worried.

"It's just that as beautiful as it is, it's not really South Tampa. Do you know what I mean?"

"Not really, no."

"It's just more . . . black, than one usually wears around here in the daytime. It would be lovely for a date to the movies."

Heads nodded.

"Yes, at that new theatre where you can have a glass of wine while you watch the movie," volunteered Sandy.

"Or you could wear it to see a jazz band or something. Aren't there jazz clubs somewhere?"

"I'm sure that there are. Good idea." I was relieved to see Constance looking hopeful rather than crushed. Mine was a tough job, I thought to myself.

"Well, here are today's handouts. I've listed a couple of athletic clubs you ought to check out. And as you might expect, I'm recommending joining the Junior League, the Yacht Club, and the Country Club. People take their kids to the Yacht Club on Friday nights and swimming at the athletic club on weekends."

"Do people actually work out at these places?" Pat asked.

"I don't have the slightest idea. Remember, you're there to meet other families like yours."

"I just mean, don't these people exercise?"

I thought about it. "Well, everybody certainly claims to. I know it's perfectly acceptable to be wearing your tennis whites when you drop the kiddies off at school. Expensive running shoes and some nifty shorts transform you into a runner. I've seen that look at drop-off too. I guess whether or not you really exercise is up to you. Buy a treadmill."

"I have a question," said Gloria.

"Yes?"

"It's not like you can just call up and join these places. How did you get in and can you sponsor us?"

I hemmed and hawed. I didn't wish to lie but they had to believe that I knew what I was talking about. I hedged: "I'm afraid you'll need the sponsorship of someone with more membership longevity to join the more exclusive clubs. I'll help you meet the right people, don't worry."

Ah, six happy faces again.

"Oh, Janice, how much do these places cost?"

I didn't even blink. "Well, as they say, if you have to ask . . ."

Chuckle, chuckle, snort, *damn*. What was that look my mom was giving me? I suddenly felt naked . . . and fake. *Damn her*. Luckily the meeting was wrapping up soon.

I avoided my mother for the rest of the morning but I was ambushed as I sat outside eating my lunch.

"Hello, dear. I spoke with Ted this morning," Marjorie began as she pulled out a chair and joined me. Marjorie had made little vegetable animals out of olives and raw carrots.

"I figured you spoke to him everyday. Was today special?"

"I talked to him about you today, dear." Marjorie hopped an olive bunny into her mouth.

I started to say something but I was interrupted by Kate's arrival on the screen porch.

"Hey all," Kate greeted us, pulling up another chair.

"Hello, dear. Do you want some salad?"

"Carrot birdies. Cool." Kate popped one into her mouth.

"Where have you been lately?" I asked Kate. "Anything new on the job front? You know, I picked up a catalog for you from the Community College."

"Why?" Kate looked genuinely perplexed.

"Why do you think?"

"I'm really not interested. I've been helping Gus with some lyrics and he thinks I'm really good. He even likes my singing voice. We may try and put a gig together."

"Oh, isn't that exciting," Marjorie exclaimed.

"Don't encourage her Mother. I'm not so sure it's her singing voice Gus is interested in."

"It's my job to encourage you girls. I am, however, having a bit of self-conflict over your consulting business, Janice."

"Thus the call to Ted. Christ, Mother. Kate can pierce her nipples, dance on a pole and take up nude hang-gliding and you do nothing but applaud. I start up a legitimate business and work hard to support myself and my daughter and you have to call in the karma police."

"You don't look happy, dear. At least Kate's musical pursuits bring her joy."

Kate got up from the table. "Speaking of karma, it's getting pretty negative around here. Maybe I'll write a song about it." She wandered off muttering lyrics: "My sister's on the upper crust of Mama's social pie – she needs some new pie filling before her aspirations die. Oh yeah, yeah."

I rolled my eyes and pushed back from the table. "Excuse me, Mom. I'm done eating."

38. Not Junior Enough, Fool

On Thursday morning, I resisted the temptation to teach Marcy about April Fools' Day. Knowing Marcy, she'd turn it into something sinister that had to be worried about all day. Come to think of it, that's exactly how I had always felt about it. Who needed to be worried about stupid practical jokes all day? Marcy would learn soon enough from her peers at St. whatever.

After dropping Marcy off at the school, I drove over to the office of the Suncoast Junior League. I'd called ahead to make sure that the person in charge of memberships would be there. In the parking lot, I found a place to park next to a small, stylish station wagon. I wondered momentarily if there was going to be a shift to smaller family cars. But a glance around the lot cured me of that notion. Behemoths all.

The Junior League's office was in a renovated home. The entrance was pretty with seasonal flowers and a perky little sign welcoming visitors unless you were a solicitor. I walked in and asked the first person I saw if I could speak to the membership coordinator. The young woman looked a little surprised but didn't hesitate to usher me down a short hallway to an office with an open door. Inside the office sat Twin Vans.

"Janice?"

"Frances?"

We stared at each other for an uncomfortable moment until Twin Vans put on her professional face. "Is there something I can help you with?" Then she looked as if she suddenly thought of something. "Don't tell me my sprinkler system is shooting water at Mr. Higgins' car again. How did you know where to find me?"

I regained my composure as well. "I'm here to inquire about membership."

"For . . .?"

"Junior League."

"I mean, who wants to join?"

Is she really that stupid? "Me. I want to join." I plopped down on a chair facing Twin Vans across her desk. Frances looked decidedly uncomfortable and yet, somehow smug.

"Actually, Janice, you needn't have come all the way down here. We have a website that explains everything."

"*Actually*, I know. I skimmed over it last night." *Lie.* "You gals really do some great charity work. But there wasn't really all the information I was looking for."

"Such as?"

"Well, you know. Aren't there social things too? Don't you have parties and stuff? I always imagined Junior League women caravanning down to the outlet mall for a shopping trip, and stuff like that. I'll bet you have great Christmas parties."

"Well, we members do become friends, of course, but the Junior League isn't just some social club."

"Right. So exactly how do you become a member?"

"You didn't read the membership information?"

"I told you, I skimmed."

"Well, for starters, you can't just apply, Janice. You have to be proposed by current members."

"Like you?"

Twin Vans squirmed. "Not just me. Really, I think you should go back and read the membership criteria."

I felt ire rising up my neck, putting a flush on my cheeks. I felt awkward enough here, out of my element, so to speak. It was one thing for Twin Vans to refuse to introduce me to her hair stylist. But she couldn't keep me out of Junior League. Could she? "What are you telling me, Frances? That I couldn't possibly have the right kinds of friends to propose my membership? I may be new to South Tampa but I'm not new to the area. I have friends, for Christ's sake. Just how exclusive is this little club of yours?"

"I didn't mean to upset you, Janice," Frances said with a smile that contradicted her message. "As I'm sure you know, we are a service organization providing volunteers and other support to causes around the entire community. This isn't some social club. And it isn't small. We actually have more than a thousand women in our organization. And I'm sure you know women, besides me, who could propose your membership."

I calmed a little.

Twin Vans continued, "It's just that if you had read the membership criteria, you might have saved yourself some time this morning."

"Again with the criteria. Am I missing a certain tattoo on my butt or something?"

"Actually, I'm sure that your rear-end tattoos are fine with our membership guidelines. But how old are you, Janice?"

I didn't want to answer the question. It just had never occurred to me before this very moment that the "Junior" in Junior League meant anything. *Oops.* "I'm thirty-six. I'll be thirty-seven in July."

Twin Vans just gazed at me.

"I'm too old, aren't I? Never mind, don't answer. I'll see you around the neighborhood, Frances." I picked up my fake alligator skin purse and hustled out the office door.

Ouch!

39. Nothing Personal

When I got home, I decided not to look up the Junior League website on my computer. What was the point? It would only underscore my embarrassment. So the Junior League wasn't just a little social club. I was still pretty sure that it attracted a lot of socialites. I would simply have to figure out a different angle to mix with the desired crowd. As for my consulting group, they were all probably too senior to join too. I'd have to let them down easy. I made a few notes to myself in a notebook and looked out the window in time to see Grace heading up my walkway.

I met her at the door. "Hi Grace. What's up?"

"Well, I wanted to say hello and invite you to something. I just got back from my Bible study class and I was thinking about how great I feel and how much you might like to come. It really doesn't matter what your religious background is."

I wanted to duck and run. Instead I offered a half-truth. "That is so thoughtful of you, Grace. But I'm already involved in a study group. We meet right here."

"That's great! I just thought you might like to meet some more of my friends. We're all in Junior League together. Hey, I should come to your Bible study sometimes. It's certainly close enough. Hee, hee."

I mulled over the possible responses. Here was this neighbor that I suspected of having an affair with my husband. *Estranged husband?* Anyway, I wasn't so sure anymore. Grace was being incredibly neighborly and obviously hobnobbed with a crowd I wanted to meet. *Point in her favor.* On the other hand, would I have that much in common with somebody who wanted to be a member of not one but two Bible study groups? *Point against her.* Then again, maybe Grace was lonely and just wanted to socialize and this was one of the ways she could hang out with people. *Point in her favor.* I could understand that impulse. With a sudden sort of epiphany, I found a way to lay the first issue to rest.

"Grace, have you been shopping for a new car? I know your old one has been giving you trouble."

Grace looked a little baffled but didn't hesitate to answer. "No. I'm keeping my clunker. Your husband Jeff made a big pitch to me to buy something from his lot. He sent me these postcards and stuff and he even talked me into test-driving a high-end sedan. As if, hee, hee. I have other money priorities right now. Why?"

And that had to be why I had seen Grace and Jeff together at the mall. "Oh nothing, really. I've been meaning to ask you since I saw you and Jeff at the mall one day. I figured he was putting on the pressure."

"You can say that again. He made me drive to the mall and go chat to my girlfriends about the car. I guess to enlist their persuasive peer powers. Whatever. You can tell Jeff I haven't bought anything from anybody else either. It's nothing personal."

"I'll be sure to mention it next time we chat." I felt a huge sense of relief wash over me. I wanted to like Grace and now I could. More than that, I could finally stop wondering if Jeff had been having an affair with her. Maybe things could still work out in the Jeff department.

If I wanted that. This news changed everything. Jeff had not left me for another woman. But he had left. We had been fighting a lot and nothing had really changed. Of course I'd been refusing any opportunity to discuss the matter. *Ugh*. Part of me desperately wanted him to come home right away. Part of me enjoyed having him live somewhere else while I figured out what I needed. No part of me wanted a divorce.

What is my problem?

40. Little Fishies

That afternoon, I picked up Marcy from school and took her directly to her first swim class at Miss Sophie's Swim Academy.

I parked around back and followed a woman and a skinny little boy around front to the entrance. The swim school was in a small, renovated house. There was still a bathtub in the bathroom. The large room overlooking the pool wasn't empty today as it had been when I'd signed up Marcy for the beginner's class. It was full of moms chatting up a storm while their little fishies finished with their lessons. It was the usual array of South Tampa moms. By now I could even recognize a few from school drop-off. And wasn't the Light Ash Blonde in the corner at book club?

"What do I do, Mommy?" Marcy asked. She was wearing a dark blue swimsuit under her cover-up. She had already slipped off her sneakers.

"When these two classes are done, they'll call for the next class and then it will be your turn." Marcy looked a little worried. "You know, I'm really proud of you that you are going to learn how to swim. I took swimming lessons when I was little too."

We waited on a chair until the other moms gathered their belongings and went over to the dressing room to greet their wet kids with towels and hugs. A couple of other children had arrived, presumably to join Marcy in the beginner class. I moved up to a seat with a better view of the pool through the windows. Marcy took off her cover-up and stood by the door until a young man in swim trunks came up and escorted her and the other kids to the pool.

I held my breath as I watched, wondering if Marcy would balk at getting into the water. Marcy hadn't spent much time in pools. Happily, Marcy didn't hesitate at all to climb down a couple of steps and sit in the water. The instructors (there were three) began singing and pouring water over the children's heads. It appeared that they were teaching the kids not to fear the water and not to wipe their eyes with their hands. Blinking the water out of your eyes appeared to be the order of the day. *Good luck.*

With Marcy engaged in her class, I had time to look around and start up a conversation with one of the other mothers. I was disappointed to see that at this time slot, there were very few moms. Marcy's class only had four kids in it today. And it was the only class at this time. As I looked around, I despaired at another realization. These weren't moms. These were nannies. Two were young foreign girls, au pairs maybe? And the other was an elderly Hispanic woman with a pile of knitting in front of her.

For the next forty minutes, I watched three swim instructors dump water on Marcy's head while knitting needles clanked on my left and the two au pairs chatted animatedly in a German or maybe Russian dialect.

For this I was paying more than one hundred dollars a month.

41. Blind Date

Grace called me that evening.

"I was thinking about you this afternoon," she said mischievously.

"I'm glad you called. Do you know anyone who belongs to the Country Club?"

"Funny you should ask. I was going to tell you about this guy I know. He's a lawyer and I've known him for a while now and I ran into him today."

"And?"

"And I was thinking that maybe you would like to meet him." Grace giggled. "He definitely belongs to the Country Club."

"Oh, God, Grace. I don't know."

"You told me you dated some loser in cowboy boots. Come on. You'll like this guy. Think of it as fun. You aren't signing a marriage contract."

"Right. I'm still married to Jeff and . . ."

"And nothing!" Grace cut me off. "You need to have some fun, Girlfriend. It will help you figure out what you want in your marriage. Besides, I gave him your number. His name is Robert and he's likely to call you this evening."

Just what I needed. More stress. "Is he good looking?"

"Very. And rich, just like you like 'em."

"Grace!"

"Don't play innocent with me, Jan Darcy." Giggle.

"Goodnight, Grace."

Robert Hammellin called shortly after nine o'clock. He sounded a little nervous on the phone and claimed to be inexperienced in the blind date department. He cracked a few dumb jokes, one of which had "banana split infinitive" as its punch line.

"I hope Grace told you about my situation," I responded. "I'm not divorced, just separated." My voice was flat and unexcited. *Who is this guy?* I hoped to scare him off. "I have a little girl. She's almost four."

"Wow, that's great. I'd like to meet her, and you, I mean – Grace said you like jazz. Would you like to come with me tomorrow night to hear this trio I read about? They're playing at a small club near the airport. You could meet me there. You know, in your own car. Then once you figure out that I'm not an axe murderer, maybe I could pick you up sometime for dinner."

I smiled. He was nerdy but perceptive. "Sure, what time?" And so I made a date with Robert Hammellin. I called Grace to let her know and Grace squealed like a schoolgirl. I didn't think to call Margaret.

All the next day, I fielded calls from Grace. What was I going to wear? When was my last manicure? Did I need to borrow some perfume? Grace had me so worked up that I almost forgot to ask a very important question. Almost.

"Grace, if this guy is so great, why aren't you dating him?"

"Oh, well, good question. He is great. I guess he's just not exactly my type."

"What?"

"He's well, hair challenged. I just can't seem to get past it."

I laughed. Baldness was not a drawback in my view. I relaxed significantly. Another balding young man had pursued me a long time ago. The memory still made me blush. Joey was one of Jeff's former colleagues who had been relentless in his puppy love for me. I'd received poetry and flowers and confessions of his desires all without Jeff suspecting a thing. I'd never once encouraged Joey, but neither had I blown the whistle. I had thought him very attractive in spite of his youth, acne and prematurely receding hairline. His very enthusiasm for me had been intoxicating. Eventually he'd transferred to another town. I still wondered about him occasionally.

Due to the circumstances of this evening's date, I did not feel particularly pressured to dress-to-kill. I had never been on a blind date in my life and I suspected that they were always doomed to failure. I didn't wear the toe-killer boots, instead settling on a sensible pair of flats to go with my skirt and blouse. Robert was meeting me straight from his office and was likely to be dressed conservatively. If nothing else, I would use the evening to find out a thing or two about joining the Country Club.

I got in the van at about seven and headed over to the club. Marjorie was reading Marcy a story when I left. I wondered what Jeff was up to that evening.

42. Jazzed

Robert Hammellin was not bald. He was a touch gray and his hairline wasn't anywhere close to his eyebrows but he was not bald. He was handsome. His suit was dark and crisp. I felt my palms begin to sweat just as I reached out to shake hands and introduce myself.

"I hope you haven't been waiting long," I said as I slid into the other side of the booth. Soft music drifted over to us from the trio in the corner. The room was lovely. It was softly lit with candles and white linens on the tables. A single red flower rested in a glass bud vase.

Robert stared at me with an intensity that unnerved me a bit. "You are beautiful. Grace neglected to mention that when she listed off all your positive attributes and convinced me to call you."

I blushed down to my toes. "You know, I was a little mad at Grace for setting me up. I've never been out with someone I haven't met before."

"It's okay to say blind date. I've been on lots of them."

"Didn't you say exactly the opposite on the phone?"

"A white lie."

"Oh," I brushed it off. "Well, I'm glad I'm here. This is a nice place. Do you come here very often?"

"Is that a pick up line?"

I blushed again. "Have you already ordered a drink? I think I'll have a glass of red wine. Maybe a little alcohol will speed up my wit so I can keep up with you."

"By all means." He motioned for the cocktail waitress and placed my order.

We spent the next couple of hours talking and listening to music. I minded my drinks since I was driving myself this evening. The bar was a perfect first date location with its live, interesting music being played softly enough to converse over. I felt my attraction growing as the evening slipped by. For his part, Robert seemed very interested. He brushed his fingers by mine a couple of times and leaned way over the table. I fretted over his tie a few times. It looked too expensive to burn up on the candle. Eventually he took my hand and we stepped out onto the very small dance floor in front of the band.

I felt warm and cozy. Robert made me feel totally at ease. I hadn't learned much about him. He'd mostly asked me a million questions about my family and Marcy and my life in general. I felt important to have somebody so interested in my life for a change. He'd even asked my about my goals and aspirations.

Promptly at nine, Robert brought the date to an end. When I'd left my house that evening, I had been sure that I'd be the one cutting out at nine o'clock pronto. I felt a little bit jolted at Robert's abrupt finish to the date that had seemed to be going so well.

"I'm very sorry, Janice, but I'm going to have to call it a night. I've got some important work to do tomorrow and I need to be fresh."

I informed him that I understood and that I needed to get back to Marcy anyway (who had better actually be in bed.) He walked me to my car and gave me a light peck on the cheek. Almost an air kiss.

"I'll call you," he said and left in his Jaguar. Not the entry-level type.

I cursed Grace all the way home. How could she have set me up with someone so perfect who would lead me on for hours just to dash me to the curb after a couple of spins on the dance floor. Did I have body odor? Did I get drunk? Did I mention Jeff even once? No, no, and no way. *Ugh*. What was the deal?

I sat up talking with Grace on the phone until past midnight, parsing each moment of the date. In the end, neither of us could figure out why it had ended with an "I'll call you."

"He really is busy all the time. He has a very successful practice. I'm sure it had nothing to do with you at all. Maybe he really is going to call." Grace tried to sound hopeful but I knew better. *Damn.* "Say, can I ask you a favor?" asked Grace.

"Of course."

"Would you mind picking up my dry cleaning for me tomorrow? It's on the corner of Kennedy and West Shore. I have to be at a thing all day tomorrow and there's a dress I really need for tomorrow night."

"No problem. I know the place. I'll get it for you first thing."

"You're a pal."

43. Session Five

Two weeks had passed since the last session. I had given everybody the week off for Spring Break. Or maybe they had given me the week off. Most everybody in the group had gone away for the week to somewhere warmer and sunnier and resort-ier, or somewhere cold, snowy and full of celebrities in ski gear. I had stayed home with Marcy doing finger paints and reading most every Dr. Seuss book in print. We'd played at the park quite a bit too because after all, if you don't already live in Florida, it's where you *want* to be for Spring Break. To break the habit of dwelling on Robert and the mysteriously busted date, I tried pain therapy. Every time I thought about Robert and his good looks and beautiful car, I bit the inside of my lip

One morning Jeff had joined us at the park. He'd brought two coffees and an apple juice. In more than three months we still hadn't moved forward or backward in our relationship. He still lived in the apartment that I had not even seen and he still called Marcy almost every day, even though Marcy wouldn't say more than two words to him on the phone. We still didn't talk about anything important and that was mostly my fault. Every time an important topic came up, I changed the subject quickly before I got sick to my stomach or started an argument.

At the park, I had finally broken down and asked Jeff if he was dating. I desperately hoped not but I didn't know whether that was because I didn't want him to be more successful at it than me, or whether that was because I still might want to keep him on the back burner for myself.

"Are you kidding?" had been his response. He'd looked crushed. "I figure all our years of marriage deserve a little time before we give up." He'd looked stricken as he asked me if *I* had been dating.

"Of course not," I had replied with my now commonplace half-truth. For the moment, it was true.

Since that day in the park, Jeff had been making more overtures to me to get together and talk about our problematic past and our future, whatever it looked like. I continued to put him off. I had been nearly frantic before that Jeff wanted to rush down the path to divorce. Now that I knew he wanted to try to work things out, I felt just as frantic (but of course, a little more secure for the moment). What *did* I want? For starters, I knew I wanted Jeff to be more like the other dads I saw in the park that morning. Dressed sharply with cell phones on their ears conducting important business, driving shiny black SUVs, making plans to take their wives out to a fabulous dinner and perhaps a show at the Performing Arts Center before going home to their large house with a pool.

I had been busily improving myself and I felt I deserved an improved position in society. *Come on Jeff! Don't make me leave you behind.*

On this Wednesday morning, I needed to focus on my job. It was session five already. Where had the time gone? Today I planned to cover a hodge-podge of subjects and then later I was going to escort them to high tea at a trendy little place in SoHo (South Howard). It seemed every city with over a few hundred thousand people had a SoHo these days.

The women arrived promptly and I led them into my living room for coffee and low-fat muffins. Constance looked like she might have dropped a few pounds. For my part, I had fallen off the dry cereal diet and was now into crunchy little soybeans. I snacked on them constantly between meals. I hadn't lost any more weight recently, but I knew I would just as soon as I gave up caffeine and alcohol (which was to say, when pigs flew).

"Good morning, everybody. Nice to see you back. My, Trudy, your tan gives you away. Which ski resort were you at?"

Trudy sported a reverse raccoon look with dark cheeks and a white mask across her eyes where her sunglasses had shielded her eyes on the slopes. She smiled. "We were in Switzerland."

The rest of the women immediately began asking her about her trip.

"I've never been to Switzerland except in summer. Was it really cold this time of year?"

"What was the exchange rate like?"

"We're thinking of going to Holland this month to see the tulips. Have any of you ever gone?"

All the women except me were leaning in close to discuss their various European vacations.

"So, how about grocery shopping?" I interrupted.

Trudy answered, "Mostly we ate at restaurants. We just stopped in to get bread, cheese and wine every afternoon for snacks. And of course divine chocolate."

A chorus of "ahs" followed the chocolate comment.

"I meant grocery shopping in little old Tampa. Come on Ladies, we have work to do."

The women all settled back in their seats but cast sidelong glances at Trudy. I felt a subtle shift in leadership taking place.

"Okay. Most everybody in South Tampa shops at Grocer's, unless you are in desperate need for a gallon of milk and you haven't had time to shower and dress. Then I would try any other store. You are likely to run into acquaintances while grocery shopping and so you always want to look your best. Especially at the Grocer's on Dale Mabry. You can get away with more at the Grocer's on Gandy."

Trudy stepped up again. "I like shopping at Save More. They have an awesome vegetable department."

A few women nodded in agreement. They were totally missing the point and it was frustrating me.

"Let's move on to magazines. Southern Living is a must and Good Housekeeping wouldn't hurt. I also take People because I've found that the conversation often turns to the subject of the entertainment industry at parties and such. Here are all the magazines I subscribe to these days." I spread out a dozen. *Wow, the subscription rate had been creeping up around my house.*

"I really like cooking magazines," said Trudy.

Was she *trying* to undermine me?

"Those are good too," I said as the rest of the group leaned in to talk about cooking with Trudy. Well, they have all known each other a long time, I reminded myself miserably as somebody brought up the idea of a cooking club. At least they had the courtesy to invite me to join. Just before the session ended at its usual time, I got a call from Marcy's school. Apparently Marcy was sitting under her rest-time blanket sobbing and they wanted me to pick her up. So much for high tea.

I excused the group and told them to have a good time at the teashop. I wondered for a minute if any of them would be back next week for the final meeting. This morning's session had bombed and it had felt faintly reminiscent of that brunch back in December.

44. Marcy's Job

"What are you upset about, Marcy?" I inquired as I drove Marcy home from school. Her teacher had been clueless as to the particular upset today but noted that Marcy had been easily upset lately. Was she sleeping okay? Were there any big changes going on at home? Were there any deaths in the family? *Is it any of your damn business?*

Marcy dabbed her eyes with a tissue. "I wanted you," she replied in a cracked voice.

"I always want to be with you too, Sweetheart, but Mommy has work to do. And you have a job too, Marcy."

"What?"

"Your job is to go to school everyday and have fun with the other kids and your teachers. You have a really good job."

"No. What's *your* job, Mommy?"

I thought hard before I answered. "You know what my job is, Marce. It's to be your mommy. And to do a good job as your mommy, I need you to spend some time at school."

"How about you pick me up at lunchtime again?"

I felt bad. In a little more than three months, Marcy had gone from a stay-at-home kid in a two-parent household to a stay-at-school-till-two kid being jockeyed between two single-parent households. The stress must be a lot for an almost-four-year-old to bear. I changed the subject.

"Marcy, Honey, remember how we talked about celebrating your birthday early this year?"

"Yes." Sniff, sniff.

"Well, your party is this weekend. On Saturday."

"Oh boy!"

I had made sure not to mention the specific date to Marcy until the day was very close. Now seemed as good a time as any. Had Marcy known sooner, she would have been unbearable with her fussing and anticipation. "It's at the park, just like you wanted."

Marcy glowed in the back seat. Marcy spent the rest of the drive home delivering a long, excited monologue about friends and cake and balloons and I forgot all about my missed tea.

45. It's My Party

The morning of Marcy's park party dawned clear, sunny and not too hot. The real warm weather was still a month away.

"Come on, Marcy, let's go pick up your cake."

I had ordered a cake from The Bakery. A very kind cake-decorating specialist had said that she would attempt to decorate a cake with dwarfs. I had paid a small fortune for the privilege.

The Bakery was nearly empty this early on a Saturday. The cake decorator wasn't working but the counter staff found our cake and rang us up. In the parking lot, I relented to Marcy's begging and we took a peek at the cake. It was chocolate cake with vanilla frosting and seven horrible little men with pick axes and angry faces. They appeared to be on their way to murder a small village. I sucked in my breath.

"Oh, Mommy, it's the part where the dwarfs come home and find Snow White."

Marcy was gleaming and it was obvious that I was not going to be able to take it back in for a quick princess makeover.

"They don't look very happy, do they? I'm pretty sure that they didn't look like this in the movie."

"Not the Disney Snow White, the *real* Snow White." Marcy got quiet for a moment. "Mommy, what does kill mean?"

"Didn't Margaret tell you all about what it means to be dead when she was at our house? And who read you the real Snow White, anyway."

"Grandma read it to me. She said it was the real Snow White without all the whitewash."

So why couldn't Marcy ask about whitewash?

Marcy continued. "Miss Margaret just said that dead means that you fall asleep forever like Snow White."

"Okay, then 'kill' means that you made somebody fall asleep forever. But it isn't a nice thing, Marcy so let's change the subject."

"I like sleeping."

"It's not the same thing, Marcy. Look, everybody and everything that's alive now will someday die. But not until they're old, so don't worry about it today, okay Honey?"

"Are you going to die, Mommy?"

"Well, someday, yes. But not until I'm really old and you are a mommy yourself."

"Are Nana and Grandma and Aunt Kate going to die?"

"A long time from now and not all on the same day, okay?"

Marcy looked scared. "Am I?"

"Not for an even longer time."

"But if I die, I won't be able to sing anymore."

"But you might turn into an angel and sing to everybody in the whole world."

"I don't want to be an angel. Angels only sing opera music and I like fast and happy music." The conversation was taking a decidedly irrational turn.

"Please, please don't worry about anything today but having a great time at your party, okay Sweetie?"

"Bah!"

"Hi Grumpy."

I had invited all the kids in Marcy's class to the party. Most of them had indicated that they were coming, much to Marcy's and my delight. I hadn't met many of the parents yet (except Gregory Storm and they had passed on the invitation). I'd decorated a couple of picnic tables at the park with festive table cloths and balloons that I'd got on sale right after Easter. Since I couldn't find anything featuring the dwarfs, Marcy had agreed that the Easter bunnies on the tablecloths looked like the forest bunnies from the movie.

Marcy and I had arrived a little later than planned at the park to set up and therefore we were stuck at two small picnic tables under a tree. All the tables under the roof area had been snagged as early as seven o'clock that morning by bleary-eyed dads who had long since finished reading their newspapers. There was no reservation system for the park's tables. I estimated that at least four birthday parties were taking place in the small park on this day. I hoped Marcy was too young to notice that the two-year-old had a bouncy castle and a professional balloon guy and that the five year old had a clown to entertain her guests. I expected an entire petting zoo to show up before too long to entertain the other four-year-old's party guests. I knew the ages of the other children because somebody was making a small fortune painting birthday banners for outdoor parties such as these.

The whole time I was preparing the juice boxes, the snacks, the goodie bags, and the plates and cups, Marcy was sulking on the slide. She was still bothered about death.

"Mama, is Daddy going to die too?"

"Yes Honey. But like I told you, not until we're all very, very old. That's a long, long time from now."

"Like forty-five minutes?"

I went over to Marcy and gave her a hug. "Sometimes, forty-five minutes is a long time. Like when you are waiting for me to take you to the park or something. But when I say that it will be a long time before Mommy and Daddy die, I mean years and years. Do you remember how hard it was to wait for Christmas? Think about that kind of waiting fifty times."

"Wow." Marcy looked a tiny bit happier which was good because the guests were starting to arrive.

"Hi, I'm Janice Darcy Pintoff and this is the birthday girl. You must be Joshua's mommy."

"Hi. Judy Steiner."

Of course at that very moment I remembered why it wasn't a great idea to decorate with Easter-ware when your child goes to a Jewish school. Bad taste, to say the least. Maybe the Steiners wouldn't notice the brilliantly colored Easter eggs bouncing around the bunnies on the tablecloth fringe. At least there were no crosses.

The rest of the guests arrived and I gave all the children balloons to play with. Marcy continued to look pensive and refused to get off the slide. The other kids all played around the other equipment and largely ignored her, which didn't seem to bother her at all. There were far more guests than I had anticipated. Nobody had informed me about the sibling phenomena. Apparently, there was some sort of algebraic calculation you had to make to determine the extra number of mouths that might show up to a party when you invite a given number of children. Of course, even the most scientific of calculations couldn't have predicted that the Carters would bring all seven of their children.

I was making a list of the extra food I would need when I heard an escalating argument near the slide.

"It comes from pigs," a little boy was yelling at Marcy.

"I know! Ham and pork chops come from pigs. They make it with their bottoms," Marcy replied.

The pork-chops-are-pig-poop argument. *Great*. Marcy had thought that up one day and I had not disabused her of the notion for fear that Marcy would have nightmares about modern slaughter practices. It looked like this little boy was about to spill the beans.

"No they don't. You have to cut the pig up into little pieces and mix it up with chemicals."

Marcy looked over to me. Her face fell when I didn't immediately overrule the boy's explanation. I went over to Marcy and tried to coax her off the slide. Marcy wouldn't budge.

"Marcy, Honey, are you okay?"

"Mommy? Do people eat animals?"

"Yes, they do. But all animals eat animals. Well, actually some are vegetarians. But we're omnivores. We eat everything. Do you want to go play ball with the other kids?"

Marcy started crying. "So the animals are all empty of life?"

"Well, yes, Honey. The ones we eat are. But it's okay, really. Why don't we talk about this at home later."

"You told me that people have to be nice to animals and take good care of them. People do not take good care of animals when they eat them!"

"Marcy, . . ."

I stopped when I realized that Marcy's gaze was suddenly riveted elsewhere. Marcy shrieked loud enough to catch everyone's attention.

"MOMMY!!! YOU SAID THAT THEY WERE JUST MAKE-BELIEVE. Aaagh!!!" Marcy screamed and cried all the way down the slide, across the park and out the gate. She stopped running and stood with her head in her hands crying by our car.

I half smiled at everyone and tried to figure out the source of my daughter's outburst. Two glances around the park and the answer was right there in front of me. On a bench near the playground was a little person. A mild looking man who didn't bear any resemblance to the murderous looking dwarfs on the cake, other than his small stature. But I could see why, under the circumstances, Marcy had been afraid.

"I'll be right back," I told everybody as I hustled after Marcy.

My daughter was practically convulsing. "Moooommmmyyyy."

Poor Marcy. Here it was her birthday party and the topics of conversation had been death and dying and animal slaughter. Here it was her party and a real life dwarf-like person had shown up to prove that everything Mommy said was a lie. Here it was her party and her daddy hadn't even been invited (he would be having a party later with Mule Slides for her real birthday).

I hugged Marcy tight. "You know, Honey, just because that man is short, doesn't mean he's a dwarf. He's just small."

Marcy just cried louder.

"Do you want to go home?"

Just then Margaret showed up with her kids.

I motioned her over. "Margaret, I think I'm going to take Marcy home. Do you mind taking over? All you have to do is collect the presents, hand out goodie bags and make sure everybody has cake. There's not enough sandwiches for everybody so don't even bother. Tell everybody I'm sorry but they all have kids. I'm sure they'll understand. Mom and Kate should have been here by now. They're bringing some more prizes. Anyway, when they show up, they can help you. You can send the leftover stuff home with them."

"So what happened?"

I rolled my eyes. "Where could I even start? I'll talk to you later. Thanks, Margaret."

"Anytime."

Once again, Margaret to the rescue.

46. Session Six

Nobody came except for Constance. Every other one, Trudy, Sandy, Pat, Karen and Gloria had found an excuse not to make it to our final session. It's not like they had asked for a refund or anything, but the message was pretty clear. Even if I saw fit to continue in my consulting business, the well of prospective clients had just dried up. Constance confirmed my fears.

"I'm so sorry, Janice. Trudy has known these gals a long time and they just tend to listen to whatever she says. At that tea that you couldn't make . . . well, she just sort of staged a coup."

"What?"

"I'm sorry, she just got to talking about how we, they, didn't need to be paying somebody for your kind of . . . information. She volunteered to take over for free. I think she's even starting a Bunko group. Sorry, really."

I felt like I'd been stabbed. Even I hadn't made my way into a Bunko group yet. Of course, was it really the same thing if you just created your own group out of whole cloth? *Hardly*!

"Constance – are you with me or against me?"

Constance didn't hesitate. "I can't stand Trudy."

"So you're with me?"

"Let's do it!"

Constance jumped up and the two of us high-fived. Then Constance got a little quiet. "I'm sorry, Janice. But what is it that we are going to do?" she asked.

I felt a resurgence of spirit. "Take South Tampa by storm, damn it!"

"You know, my husband and I haven't found a house yet."

"Then that will be our first priority. Who's your agent?"

"Uhm, well . . . sorry."

"Never mind. We'll find you one today. Come on Constance, we have a house to buy. And quit apologizing all the time, will you?"

And so session six became a house-hunting expedition for Constance and her family, a husband and twin boys aged two and a half.

I drove us around in my van. "Constance, I want to tell you that whatever your budget, the neighborhood you choose is far more important than the size of the house or even the newness of the house. I've been watching a lot of *Trading Spaces . . .*"

"What?"

"A redecorating show and I've seen what you can do on a small budget. Anyway, you should probably restrict your looking to my neighborhood, Beach Park, and maybe Hyde Park and New Suburb Beautiful. Lots of name people live in big beautiful houses in other neighborhoods and on Davis Island and such, but you really can't go wrong with the neighborhoods I just mentioned."

Constance looked concerned. *Poor Constance*, I thought. Trudy and her gang probably discriminated against her because she was a little overweight and not so outgoing (or pushy?). But I liked that about her.

"So Constance," I continued, "about what is your price range? I don't mean to get personal, I just need to know so I can help out." I felt bad for having to ask. I knew how it felt to be scraping.

Constance blushed. "Of course any purchase will have to be contingent on the sale of our current house, but Dan and I have discussed a range of $800,000 to $1,000,000."

Now I blushed. "Well, okay then." *Hmmm, still waters run deep.* "So exactly what does your husband do for that company?"

"He's the President."

Ahhh. Sorry indeed!

47. Second Date

Robert Hammellin finally called. It had been nearly four weeks since our first and only encounter. Grace hadn't had any more insights for me regarding Robert nor had she arranged any more blind dates. She had, however, managed to get me to pick up her dry cleaning on a weekly basis. I didn't mind. Grace had been really busy lately and the dry cleaning exchange allowed us some time to catch up occasionally. Wait until Grace heard about this. I remained frosty on the phone as I listened to Robert's explanation.

"So I'm really sorry, Janice. I finally meet somebody interesting and the next thing you know I'm swept up into an attempted hostile takeover and my life is not my own. I guess that's why they pay me the big bucks. Strike that. I guess that's why *I* pay me the big bucks." Hah, hah.

So I invited him over.

It was another Friday night. Robert arrived after Marcy had gone to bed so that I could avoid any uncomfortable explanations (okay, lies) to Marcy. I had dressed more carefully this time in black silk and almost naughty heels. I'd dimmed the lights and placed a few candles around, trying to recreate the ambiance of that bar. Robert looked handsome in a trim sweater with some black and white checked slacks. His distinguished hair was slicked back with just a hint of gel. He smelled great.

"Wine?" I asked.

"Love some," Robert replied. When I returned, I sat next to Robert on the couch and clinked my glass against his.

"Here's to a not so blind date."

"Cheers." Robert somehow managed to sip from his glass without taking his eyes off of me. I was transfixed.

"I really enjoy what you are doing in this room," Robert said, finally taking his gaze away from me.

"Thank you," I replied, resisting the urge to discuss *Trading Spaces* again.

"What you really need now is some great art. Maybe Asian influenced prints. And you know you can get some really nice slipcovers for those chairs. Did you inherit them from your grandmother or something?"

I made quick mental notes as Robert continued to offer opinions about my décor. Before tonight, I'd thought I was basically done in the living room and ready to move on to the master bedroom that was still furnished with Jeff's old bachelor pad furniture. Black lacquer and mirrors. *Yuk*. Would Robert be offering me opinions in the bedroom as well? I nearly hyperventilated. I offered him some cheese.

"Thank you. Is this French brie?"

"Hmmm, probably, yes, I think so."

Robert smiled a little and popped the morsel into his mouth. Once again we fell into an easy conversation. Instead of asking about me, this time Robert went on and on about himself. He'd led a fascinating life replete with foreign travel, top-notch education, and casual acquaintance with celebrity. *Why on Earth was this man single?* I was enchanted. He'd even been gracious to Marjorie when she'd passed by the room on her way to the kitchen for some more hot water for tea. I had managed to parlay the reason for my mother's presence into one of charity on my part.

Once again, however, Robert ended the date abruptly. This time at ten. I wondered if I had been totally imagining the chemistry between us. He apologized again and promised that we would get together again soon. I was nearly out of my mind until he uttered those magic words, "how about next Saturday night? I'll pick you up at seven." He gave me a long, delicious kiss on my front doorstep. "I'd better run while I still have the will to leave."

I watched him go out to his car and nearly collapsed with glee when I saw Twin Vans out in front of her house fiddling with a sprinkler. Twin Vans *had* to have seen the Jaguar. And the kiss. There she was in her hair rollers and stocking feet, watering her grass illegally on a Friday after dark. Water restrictions were still in force and Friday was definitely not one of Twin Vans water days. Had I felt less magnanimous, I might have dialed up the water commission to report the crime. Instead I called Grace.

48. Third Date?

I spent the next week shopping like mad. First I went to Saks and charged a seven hundred dollar dress for my date with Robert. I enlisted the help of Grace who picked out something black with a minute print on it. When I got the dress home, closer inspection revealed that the print was of hourglasses and globes, not mere geometric figures. How interesting and expensive looking, I thought.

None of my bargain outlet shoes were going to do the trick so I decided on the dominatrix boots again. It felt like a thrifty, responsible decision in light of the splurge on the dress. I also borrowed jewelry from Constance who kept more expensive baubles strewn about on her dresser than I had ever owned in my life.

Constance also showed me around her favorite art galleries. Using the latest in a string of new credit cards, I purchased several new paintings by local artists and a few art prints of Asian influence from a dealer in Ybor City. To go with the new art, I stopped into a gourmet chef's shop and bought a small Japanese sake set and a new marble cheese server. I planned to have Robert in for a quick drink before we went on our date. I wanted to impress him with my purchases. *Didn't sake seem consummately sophisticated?*

By Friday, I was positively giddy. I'd been reliving that kiss all week long. Even Marcy's new insistence on becoming a vegetarian didn't bother me. I took Marcy to the health food section at Grocer's and let her pick out some delicious soy-based protein alternatives and some enriched rice milk. I figured the vegetarian thing would pass soon. Hadn't the whole dwarf thing pretty much evaporated with the recent purchase of the *Toy Story* videos?

Friday evening after Marcy was in bed, I got out the purple wax goo and removed my mustache. The sting was still drawing tears to my eyes when I got the phone call.

"Hello?"

"Hey, Janice." It was Grace, but she sounded really low.

"What's the matter? You sound dismal. I have your clothes . . ."

"I don't know how to tell you this."

"What? Oh God, did your mom die?" Grace's mother had been very ill lately.

"No. Robert called me today. What a jerk."

I did not like the direction this conversation was taking. "What did he say?"

"He wanted me to explain to you why he's canceling your date with him tomorrow night."

I laughed. "I suppose he's in the middle of another hostile takeover. I swear I will never date another lawyer. I guess he was too chicken to call me himself."

Grace hesitated. "Yes, sort of. Janice, he doesn't want to go out with you at all."

"He said that?" I sat down hard on my bed. Jeff's bed, the one with the black lacquer. Tears spilled out over my fingers on the phone.

"I'm so sorry, Janice. I never should have set you up with him. He's so picky. I just thought that the two of you would have some fun. I didn't dream that he'd be too much of a jerk to end things on his own. Imagine him calling me to break it off with you."

"Did he say why?"

"Like I said, he didn't want to be the one to hurt your feelings."

"No, I mean, did he say why he wanted to end things?" I sniffed loudly.

"Do you really want to hear what he said? Remember, he's a jerk. A typical jerk male." Grace forced out a trademark giggle.

"What did he say?"

"He said that you weren't worldly enough and that there was no point in continuing now that he felt that way."

Ouch.

"Grace, will you do me a favor?"

"Sure. What is it?"

"Will you kick him in the balls for me next time you see him?"

"Hee, hee. Done!"

Instead of getting ready for my big date, I spent Saturday finding out that the galleries would not accept returns of the artwork I'd purchased. Luckily the sake set went back without question. I debated long and hard about the dress and finally decided it was a sign of good positive thinking to hang onto it. After all, if I returned the dress, I was really admitting to myself that I would never have a reason to wear it. Who needed that kind of negativity? Constance agreed with me. She kept me company most of the day. Marjorie took care of Marcy. It was Constance who had the idea that really perked up my spirits.

"Janice, Honey, I'm sorry but we need to have a party."

"Can I invite my class?" Marcy asked, obviously eavesdropping from the family room.

"No, Sweetie. Miss Constance is talking about a party for grown-ups."

Constance shook her head. "Oh, sorry, I mean let's invite kids too. Great idea, Marcy. We'll make it a sort of neighborhoody, family thing with fireworks, and alcohol. I like it."

"Me too," chimed in Marjorie passing by with a snack for Marcy.

"Me three," I said.

"Me four!" yelled Marcy. "Can Daddy come?"

PART III: QUELLE PROBLEMES
(Yikes.)

YOU'RE INVITED

<u>TO</u>:   A Fourth of July Party

<u>WHERE</u>:   Janice Darcy's House

<u>WHEN</u>:   Saturday, July 4
7:00 pm

<u>BRING</u>:   Your favorite beverage!

<u>RSVP</u>:   555-6871

49. Party Plans

Constance helped me plan for the Fourth of July party. Mostly, Constance invited a lot of her new neighbors on the street she'd moved to, just a few blocks over from me. Everything there was a lot larger: the lot sizes, the houses, the cars, and the incomes. Only the trees were of similar scale. We'd decided to hold the party at my house though, because Constance was still getting settled into hers. Paint crews, landscape designers, and contractors of various ilk were all day swarming Constance's property. Besides, I was the one who needed to hostess a successful party.

During the weeks leading up to the party, I had spent every minute that I could making small improvements to my own modest estate. Painfully cognizant of the fact that my economics forced me into being a do-it-yourselfer, I'd agreed to let my older neighbor behind my house, Mr. Simmond, park his work van on my driveway in the afternoons when he was home. He was retired but kept up a furniture repair business for amusement. The plain white van could pass for any kind of contractor's car and I noticed that even Twin Vans had become curious about it, craning her neck as she parked her own van in the driveway across the street.

"I'm having work done," I would shrug noncommittally as I waved to my neighbor. It only lasted until Mr. Simmond's driveway had been repaired but it was long enough for effect. In the meantime, I painted my living room a new designer color called simply "Grass." I made a few other home improvements as well but I'd sold off the last stick of my aunt's antique furniture and was beginning to wonder how I would keep up with the minimum monthly payments that were coming in. The new credit card offers had dried up so I could no longer simply move balances around. After the party, I simply would have to think up a new career for myself. Naturally I hadn't even raised the prospect of my mom moving out of my house lately. I needed the modest rent I collected from my mom for the mortgage.

I had kept Marcy in school for the month of June so that she could get to know her new teacher for next year. She was going to be spending another year at the Jewish Family Center School. Unsurprisingly, Marcy had not been welcomed into the halls of St. X. For weeks, I had wondered if Marcy hadn't been put on some private school black list because St. Y wouldn't interview her and even St. Z, who had already declined to interview Marcy, had called up just to make sure I understood that their classes were full for next year. *Yes, thank you, message received loud and clear.*

I would have been more upset by the developments if it weren't for the fact that I had an easy excuse to offer – Marcy's latish birthday. I told everyone that those ignorant private schools had simply insisted that Marcy wait another year. Incensed, I was looking at other alternatives. Other moms would nod in understanding, especially those who had boys with summer birthdays. In truth, I had no idea why Marcy's application had been rejected. I had a sneaking suspicion it had a lot to do with parental income and ability to donate extra money, but I'd never be able to prove it.

On this Thursday before the big Fourth of July party, my mission was two-fold: find the perfect patriotic outfit for the party and stop in at one of the myriad fireworks stands and get a few dazzlers for the kids to enjoy.

My first task was the hardest, even though I'd been told that as a technical matter, fireworks were against the law in Florida unless you were using them for some approved agricultural purpose, like scaring birds or something. To get around that technicality, all you had to do was sign some photocopied piece of paper stating that your purpose for purchasing the fireworks was on the up-and-up. Right, like mint colored sparklers and smoky little worm things were going to scare away a flock of hungry crows.

For an outfit, I felt compelled to outdo Twin Vans. Grace had agreed that we couldn't very well have the party without inviting her. I owed Frances a party. But I knew that Twin Vans would turn up in some showstopper of an outfit. She'd probably strap a fireworks-spewing volcano to the top of her head and hire a marching band to follow her around and play Sousa tunes. The one thing I was sure that Twin Vans couldn't pull off was subtle, sexy and sophisticated. That would have to be my look. I spent the entire morning looking for just the right thing and finally settled on a strappy little number that was just right for the expected heat index.

Sizzling.

50. Raccoons Are Nocturnal

On my way home from shopping, I picked up Marcy from school. It was the last day of the June session so I ran into the office to sign Marcy up for another month. I had just signed the check when Marcy's class came out to the front. Marcy was in the back dragging her lunch bag along behind her. Her eyes were red-rimmed and her cheeks blotchy.

"Marcy, Honey, what's the matter? You're such a droopy girl today."

Marcy's teacher, a smallish woman with blonde hair and a large dimple, smiled worriedly at me and nodded me over to a private corner while the assistant took Marcy and the rest of the class outside to wait for the other moms.

"What's wrong with Marcy?"

Marcy's teacher sucked in her lips and creased her brows. "I was going to ask you the same thing. She's been crying everyday at the drop of a hat and she's been very apathetic about everything. She doesn't seem to want to try anything new. I have to say, the other kids are starting to just ignore her most of the time. Have there been any big changes at home?"

I tried to smooth my hackles but it was impossible. Who was this pucker-faced woman kidding? Marcy had never been apathetic about anything in her life. For a brief moment, I thought about stopping payment on the check I'd just written for the July session. *Don't give in!* "Well, as I'm sure you know, Miss Darla, Marcy's daddy is temporarily living outside the home."

"That's been since December, right?"

"Well, yes, but I expect we'll have some resolution soon. I'm sure Marcy has been a little upset but she's been handling things very well when she's at home. I can't imagine what might be upsetting her here. Is she getting plenty of stimulation? Marcy can read, you know. Maybe she's just bored."

"Maybe," Miss Darla said without conviction. "We'll have to see how it goes."

What was that supposed to mean?

"Marcy, I got us some fireworks for Mommy's party Saturday night. Isn't that exciting? You can help me." I glanced to the back seat where Marcy looked sullen and more than a little dirty. "Marce, what did you get into at school? You're a dirty doggy today." I smiled with all my heart at my unhappy daughter.

"I hit Doug with a stick and he threw dirt on me."

I nearly wrecked the car. *Marcy hit somebody?* So uncharacteristic. Maybe Marcy was struggling to become more assertive. She had always been such a passive little child. Perhaps I just needed to show her some appropriate assertive behavior. In a weird way, I felt a little proud of Marcy.

"Marcy, you know what I think? I think we need to get some ice cream."

Marcy brightened. "Yes!"

We stopped in at a small ice cream parlor where Marcy spent close to fifteen minutes deliberating about the flavor she should pick. Never mind that I had a thousand things to do to get ready for the party. I calmed myself and let Marcy take her time. By the time Marcy picked, I was getting edgy again. When the girl behind the counter delivered the wrong flavor, I lost it.

"Jesus, I can't believe that with only two customers in the whole store, you can't get the flavor right. She asked for Caramel Nut Swirlee. What is this, Toffee?" I shoved the cone back across the counter.

"I'm sorry. It's my first day. Some of the flavors look alike. I'll be happy to make a new cone."

"Yes, do that, and try reading the labels."

The girl hurried off to get a new cone. Marcy stood mutely near the glass, gazing at some frozen bananas dipped in chocolate. She pointed a grubby little finger at them.

"No, Marcy! You already took forever deciding on the ice cream flavor. You can't change your mind now."

"Mommy, do monkeys like chocolate?"

"How the hell should I know? Oh, well, if it's on a banana, I guess they probably do. But it might be bad for them like it is for dogs." I felt guilty for snapping at Marcy.

"Is it like a poisoned apple? Would the monkeys never wake up until somebody kissed them?"

"Thank you," I said to the counter girl as I got the replacement cone. "Maybe it is," I said to Marcy. That seemed to satisfy her and we went outside to a little table where Marcy could lick her cone.

Marcy still looked a little low so I tried to tease her out of her slump. "Here comes a raccoon . . . it's going to eat your ice cream . . . watch out!" I leaned over and took a lick off the top of Marcy's cone.

"Mommy, raccoons are nocturnal," replied Marcy without even looking up.

Who had sucked all the fun out of my daughter?

51. Full Calendar

Constance and I got lucky with the weather. There were no thunderstorms in the forecast for party night. I spent the entire day doing last minute chores and hanging streamers of red, white and blue on my back porch. Constance was running around and picking up food, wine and cake orders. Kate had volunteered to fetch the beer. Grace was busy, as usual, but did manage to drop off some ice and fetch her own dry cleaning for a change. The whole dry cleaning thing was beginning to remind me about running to the locker for Polly Hanson back in junior high. It wasn't as if Grace ever picked up my dry cleaning.

"So Marcy's teacher couldn't be more specific?" Grace asked as she dumped a bag of ice into a cooler.

"No. I think she was trying to blame me for Marcy's trouble at school. I felt like telling her that Marcy is a dear at home and that maybe the trouble was with her teacher."

"Why didn't you?" Grace giggled.

"Well, actually, I kind of did. But I had to be subtle. I don't want her to take anything out on Marcy."

"Where is Marcy?"

"She's watching a movie. Maybe I should check on her, now that you mention it."

"Great. I'll see you gals later. Ciao!" Grace slipped away.

Constance and I went inside where the air was considerably cooler. It was nice that our party was not going to get rained out, however, we would also miss the cooler air that typically followed a summer storm. Marcy was on the couch with a blanket on her lap. She was sucking on a couple of fingers.

"When did she start that?"

"Beats me. I've never seen her do it before. Come on, I want to show you my new dress for tonight." Constance and I headed upstairs. My closet doors were wide open. I fished out my new dress and held it up against my body for Constance to admire.

Constance's eyes lit up. "Did you get that at Dillard's? I have the exact same nightie."

I looked down at the silken, spaghetti strapped number I'd purchased the other day. It hadn't been on display in the lingerie section. I had found it with a display of patriotic stuff in the Misses department. *Nightie*? It was china blue with small, squishy looking stars and soft red stripes on the bodice. "I guess you could sleep in it, but I'm pretty sure it's not a nightgown. I found it near other dresses and shirts and stuff. And yes, I did get it at Dillard's."

"Well, it's pretty comfortable as a nightie. Do you have shoes?"

"Check these out." I pulled out a pair of heels with red silk ties on top.

"Very sexy. Are you dressing for anybody special?" Wink, wink.

"Noooo," I said with exaggeration. We both knew I was thinking about the only single male that we knew was coming to the party. He was Constance's neighbor on the east side of her new house. He was a doctor of some sort and not too recently divorced.

"Well just remember you're busy tomorrow night. We're going to that scrapbooking party, remember? At Joan's? And you're busy next Saturday with Bunko. Did you ask your friend Margaret if she wanted to sub?"

I shook off the question. Had I really offered Margaret as a Bunko substitute? Margaret wouldn't be able to come. How would she get a sitter? Margaret wasn't even invited to my own party tonight. She didn't live in the neighborhood. When we went back downstairs to the kitchen, I glanced at my calendar. I hadn't thought about anything past today but now that Constance mentioned it, I was pretty busy. Sunday was the scrapbook party. Marcy was spending the afternoon with Mule Slides. Monday was a school holiday so Marcy was going to Busch Gardens with her dad and I had scheduled a hair appointment with the woman who cut Grace's hair. Tuesday was Constance's friend's cooking club. I was getting a try-out. Also, Marcy had a play date with Alyssa from school. And swim class. Wednesday was a birthday luncheon, Thursday was Grace's bible study (although I still had yet to show up to one) and Marcy's swim class, Friday was some sort of volunteer lunch-counter thing Constance had dragged me into and Marcy had dance class, and of course Saturday night was Bunko. Book club was the week after that, and on and on and on.

52. Wait Till It Gets Dark

Guests began to arrive at about half past seven. *Fashionably late*. All except for Twin Vans. She had scurried over with her husband precisely at seven. I figured that Twin Vans wanted to check out the decorations and the food. Luckily, Constance had insisted on having the food catered from one of the best places in town. The wine was similarly of top quality, or so I presumed, not knowing a heap of a lot about wine. Twin Vans had brought her own bottle of champagne and was wearing a red leather halter-dress with red, white and blue sandals.

"Oh, hello *Francesss*," I cooed. Air kiss, air kiss.

"Thank you so much for inviting us, *Janissss*. You remember my husband, don't you?" Twin Vans gestured at the short, balding man over her shoulder. "We brought some champagne to celebrate."

I felt alarm. "Sounds great. I love champagne. It wouldn't be the Fourth of July without it!" *Shut up, Janice, you sound lame.*

"Ah, hah hah," Twin Vans laughed. "Actually, I'm not talking about that. We have our own news to celebrate. But I'm saving the announcement for later."

Immediately I looked at Twin Van's stomach. Flat. Besides, one didn't usually toast a pregnancy with alcohol, did they? What could it be then? I immediately regretted having invited this scene-stealing, attention-grabbing, over-the-top bitch that had obviously shown up just to steal my thunder. *Growl.*

"Well, I guess you know where you can stick that champagne, then, don't you?" I looked innocently at Twin Vans whose eyebrow now kissed her hairline in alarm. "There's a cooler with ice on the back porch, of course. Make yourselves at home."

"Oh, are we going to be outside most of the time?" Twin Vans looked alarmed and I could guess why. That leather was going to be hot, hot, hot on this breezeless evening.

"*Actually*, I thought about having fireworks in my family room but I was worried about the smell. How would I ever get that sulfur odor out of my carpet? So I settled on the back yard." I laughed. Twin Vans forced a laugh too. Mr. Twin Vans stayed mute. Constance came downstairs and rescued our awkward trio. I led the Twin Vans outside and I couldn't help but notice the large glittery hair bow with blinking lights that Twin Vans sported on her bun. *Where is the battery?*

I smoothed my dress and hovered around the front door waiting for the rest of the guests. When there was a good crowd out back, I left front door duty and circulated in the crowd making sure that everyone had drinks and food and proper introductions. The single Doctor wasn't there yet but Constance assured me that he planned on coming. The din on the back porch was nothing compared to the whooping and yelling in the yard. Several kids were chasing around with water balloons. Not everybody had brought his or her kids, and that was a good thing. As it was, there were at least eight or nine urchins screaming in the twilight.

"Don't waste those sparklers, kids," I yelled. "Wait till it gets dark."

Kate and Gus showed up with a guitar. I had reluctantly agreed to let them play a few tunes sometime during the party. Kate, of course, viewed it as a way of paying me back for letting her live there, etc. I, of course, viewed it as yet another huge favor for Kate. I planned to stick them in a dark corner of the screen porch after everyone was good and soused. *Screw the bad karma*, I said silently to my mother who was just coming out the back door.

"Hi mom," I said politely. I was too excited about the party to be annoyed with my mother right now.

"Hi dear. Has Margaret arrived yet?"

I glared at my mother. "Margaret's not coming, Mom."

"Yes she is. I invited her myself."

"You what?" The information cut sharply on my nerves. Now I would have to concoct some fantastic excuse for having neglected to invite Margaret myself. "Thanks a fucking lot, Mom. It's not your party."

"Well, you might as well know that I also invited a new friend of mine to this party-that-is-not-mine."

"Who?" I asked quietly, knowing the answer already.

"A woman I met at bonsai club."

"Mother, how could you?"

My mom just smiled. "We're planning on starting a nude lesbian limbo dance if things get a little boring."

I failed to speak so my mother continued. "Don't worry dear. Your friends will like Lois and so will you. She's just a friend. You really need to relax. Ted suggests . . ."

I cut her off. "Fuck Ted. Fuck Lois. Fuck fuck. God, Mom. You really are a piece of work."

"Honey, I know how comfortable you are resenting me but it's time you let it go. I love you and Marcy and I want the two of you to have some happiness. You must quit wearing your mantle of resentment."

"A Ted-ism, I presume?"

"No. Pure me. You keep pushing away the people who love you the most."

I clapped my hands. "Bravo, Mom. Your timing couldn't be better. All my friends are here for a party and you're giving me a lecture."

"All your friends, Janice?" Marjorie looked around. "Well, Margaret will be here soon. Just thought you should know." She turned around and went back into the house.

53. Make A Happier Story

I don't know exactly when Margaret arrived. I saw her and Marjorie and the Lois woman on the porch and managed to circle widely around them. The single doctor didn't arrive until nine thirty. Nobody heard him knock because everyone was out back sloshing down cocktails and beer. The red wine remained untouched. Too hot. The doctor introduced himself to me after finding Constance and ascertaining which person was the host of the party.

"Thank you so much for hosting this neighborhood party. I'm Todd, Conny's neighbor." He handed me a small bouquet of colored roses.

"Conny? You call her Conny?"

"Yeah, but she hates it so I wouldn't pick up the habit if I were you."

"Too funny. I'm Janice, of course. These flowers are beautiful, Todd. But you didn't have to bring anything."

"I know. But I'm late and I apologize best with flowers, roses in particular." He captivated me with a broad grin and a slight head tilt. "You look familiar. Did I meet you at the Fruit Ball?" He was trying to place me. "That's a beautiful dress you have on," he added.

I just stared. Todd was taller than Jeff, maybe six foot two. His hair was dark and movie-starry. I supposed he was about fifty but he looked much younger. Constance had told me that he was divorced with no children.

"Thank you." I was about to launch into a conversation when Grace squirmed her way over to where the two of us were standing. I hadn't seen much of Grace but now she tugged insistently on my arm.

"Todd, this is my friend and neighbor Grace Swingler. Have you two met?" I gave a cross look at Grace but couldn't extract my arm from Grace's grip. Grace gave the doctor a flirty grin and pulled me away.

"Pleasure," Todd said with enthusiasm as Grace and I backed away.

"Grace, what is it?" I asked.

"Your dress. It is completely see-through when you stand in front of those little tiki lights. Something about the angle. Are you sure that's not a nightgown? Constance thought it might be."

I looked down at my dress but in the dark corner of the patio, there was no discernable sheerness. "I'm sure, Grace. Thanks, I guess." I looked back over to Dr. Todd and blushed at the idea that he'd been looking straight through my clothing. He indicated that he was heading back inside and I resisted the urge to follow him straight away. Instead I circulated through the crowd, avoiding my mother, Margaret, and all light sources as I went. As I neared the back door, a smaller set of hands tugged at my skirt.

"Mommy?"

"Hi, Sweetie. Have you been having a good time?" I looked at Marcy and the answer was obvious. No, she had not been having a good time. She was dirty, teary-eyed, and obviously in the midst of some crisis.

"What's the matter, Marcy?"

Marcy just frowned at me, squinching up her eyes until she could squeeze out another tear.

"Marcy, Honey, if you don't use your words, I'll never know what's the matter." I felt impatient. I wanted to talk to the doctor. But I wanted to console Marcy more.

"It's just so upsetting," Marcy finally squeaked out.

"What? What is so upsetting?"

"The whale," Marcy sobbed, letting tears flow freely down her dirt-streaked face.

This wasn't going to be over soon. I took a deep breath and measured my voice so as not to sound impatient. "What whale, Marcy? Tell me about it."

Marcy held up a drawing that looked like pink and purple circles with a small triangle on one side. *The tail?*

"Mommy, this is the whale." Marcy pointed at the circles. "It lived a long time ago when there weren't any people, like the animals in the Mickey bulb. So he's not alive anymore."

The Mickey bulb was a reference to EPCOT Center where we'd gone on a ride in the big dome thing and seen prehistoric animals. "That's cool, Marcy. I like how you drew a blue tail."

Marcy just stared and pointed at her picture. Her chin quivered.

"What's wrong? Did you use the wrong colors?" I grasped at any explanation.

"Noooo," Marcy cried. "It's just the whale. I miss him."

I gave Marcy a big hug. She was obviously still dealing with the concept of death. "Maybe it's just a magic spell, Honey. Why don't you give him a kiss?"

"Mommy, this is just his picture. This is not a *real* whale." Marcy cried louder.

"Fine. Whatever. Marcy, why don't you pretend that this is a picture of a modern whale presently living happily in the Atlantic Ocean with all his friends? You drew him, you can make up a happier story if you want." I felt exasperated.

"Noooo, I can't!" Marcy stomped her feet for emphasis.

"Marcy, we're going to do some more fireworks in a minute. Won't that be fun? Why don't you go play for a few minutes and I'll come get you when we're all set up."

Marcy gave me a cold look and then marched away with her nose up in the air. *Are little girls hardwired with that look?*

I went out back where Kate and Gus were just setting up for their "gig." Since their only accompaniment was an acoustic guitar, it took them no time at all to get started. I was surprised at how tuneful my sister sounded. And preachy. The lyrics were for me:

> "I don't need another mother,
> sister,
> I don't need another guide . . .
>
> I've got my own way of seeing
> And I can see you like to
> hide . . .
> Behind your little fancies
> and your mortgage and your
> pride.
>
> I don't need another mother,
> sister,
> Be a mother to your own.
> I don't need another mother,
> sister,

Leave my hopes and dreams
alone.
La, la, la, la, la . . ."

Christ.
I went inside.

54. One Less Tree

Back outside, Grace was already drunk when I finally caught up with her.

"Whoa, what are you drinking, girlie?"

"Lemon gumdrop slurps," Grace belched. "Hee, hee."

"What the hell are those?" I felt irritated with Grace's over-the-top good humor.

"Wanna try one?"

"Not a chance. Hey, do you think we should do the rest of the fireworks now?" I didn't know why I was even bothering to ask. Grace was toasted. I just wanted somebody to help me out with the little fireworks show. Just then, the doctor came back outside carrying two cocktail glasses. I looked at Grace whose face grew even more flushed.

"Doctor's orders?" Grace asked as Dr. Todd delivered her drink. She giggled tremendously. It wasn't for my benefit.

"Excuse me," I murmured as I quickly departed. I ducked my head, embarrassed by the fact that my eyes had watered up. I retreated to the far side of the patio through throngs of people I didn't even know. Constance and her husband were laughing with another couple about some obviously hilarious story. I longed to pull Constance aside and ask for her advice about the single Doctor but I figured "Conny" would just laugh it off and tell me to get in there and fight for him. But I couldn't. Not because I lacked the self-regard, but because all of a sudden, I didn't know why I should. All I knew about him was that he was good looking and a professional. And apparently a mover and a shaker, judging from the way he was chatting up Grace.

I scanned the crowd. What did I know about any of these people besides the brands of clothing they were wearing? I had made myself an expert on that, if nothing else. I stood and stared like a frozen statue amidst a room full of people who didn't see me. I had the strange sensation that I was inside a movie set rather than at a real party. Even my own house seemed like a set at the moment.

An announcement from the Twin Vans shook me out of the moment.

"Hi everyone," Ms. Twin Vans shouted, a glass of champagne in her hand. "We have a little news." Twin Vans shared a private smile with her husband. "We're moving!"

"Not out of Beach Park?" somebody yelled.

"Never!" Twin Vans laughed.

A hurrah rose up over the patio. Everyone rushed to shake hands with the Twin Vans. I was confused. Hadn't they just refinished their kitchen? When the huggers and hand-shakers had cleared away, I went over to Frances to ask where they were moving.

"Azeele."

"The street?" Azeele was right around the corner.

Twin Vans ignored my stupid question. "We bought a tear-down. They're starting construction next week. Forty-five hundred square feet." Twin Vans was too excited to be smug. "My husband got a promotion this year. Oh, and did I tell you that he's going to be in a krewe? I guess it's just our year." *Okay, that was smug.*

I felt numb. Again. *When was the last time I'd really felt something other than irritation?* I wandered over to the vacant porch swing and contemplated what I had just heard. The fact that the Twin Vans were moving didn't bother me in the slightest. It was the crowd's reaction that had me in a twist. Everybody had been so happy, no, *congratulatory*, after the announcement. These people didn't even really know Frances and her husband. What they did know was that they lived on this street. My street. They were congratulating the Twin Vans on moving off this street. Hurray, the Twin Vans were finally moving on up. I had never kidded myself that I lived on the toniest street in Beach Park, but come on, if around the corner on Azeele is so far *up*, how *down* must my own street be? I felt low.

"Hey there," Margaret announced as she approached me on the swing.

"Hey."

"What's bugging you?"

"Life."

"So what's new," Margaret dropped sarcastically. It wasn't a question. She sat down by me on the swing.

"That bitch Frances really pisses me off."

"What do you care about her?"

"Good question. Say Margaret, I'm really sorry I didn't invite you tonight. I actually thought I had sent you an invitation. Good thing Mom covered for me."

"No you didn't."

"Didn't what?" I faced Margaret.

"Didn't even plan on sending me an invitation. Your mom didn't cover for you. She invited me as her friend."

"Margaret, I don't know . . ."

"Oh shut up, Janice. If I didn't like your mom so much, I wouldn't be here, even if you had sent me an invitation."

"What are you talking about?"

"For some unknown reason, I still think of you as a friend but you are pushing it, Lady. If you haven't noticed, I don't care what you wear, who your other friends are, or what brand of car you drive. But lately you're only friendly with the people who you believe do care about all that crap. I know you've been pushing away your mother all your life but in the last few months you've also pushed away your husband, your best friend, your sister and your daughter."

I reflexively defended myself regarding Marcy. "Don't even try to bring Marcy into this." I was angry with Margaret. And myself. And about everybody else right at the moment. *My daughter has started sucking her fingers and I didn't even notice. Maybe Margaret's right.*

"Okay, it's not really about Marcy. I just threw her in so you'd listen to me. Here she comes. I'm going to go find your mom."

I didn't respond. Marcy was on her way over so I wiped away the lone tear clinging to my lashes.

Marcy climbed up onto the swing with me.

"Hi Mommy."

"Hi Sweetie. Boy, you are really getting to stay up late tonight."

"Can we do fireworks now?"

I perked up. Twin Vans had stolen a little limelight for the moment but I could get it back. I had a nice array of fireworks to set off in the front yard.

"Come on, everybody. Grab your drinks and we'll go around to the front for some fireworks. I only have a few but they're really great."

Perhaps I was reading something into their faces, but I wondered if they didn't all look a little annoyed at this disruption. Thanks to Twin Van's krewe mention, they'd all started discussing the past Gasparilla season, something I had managed to learn little about. It depressed me to acknowledge that there were whole layers of society out there that I had yet to even discover, let alone worm my way into. It made my little party seem insignificant, to say the least. But I stuck with the plan and got the crowd to troop out to the front and line up along my driveway.

I lit a couple of volcano things in unison. They spewed colored fire and the kids jumped and clapped. Marcy looked ecstatic so I went ahead and lit a couple more. As I backed away, a bottle rocket flew over my head. *Who brought those?*

Although Marcy continued to watch the scheduled program, everybody else was now clamoring to have a turn setting off a rocket. It appeared that Mr. Twin Vans had brought them. Truman and Mary Blythe were assisting him.

Anger swelled inside me. Who did these people think they were? Drunken partiers laughed and fought over who got to light the next fuse. Even Constance was in the thick of it. Another rocket zoomed over my head, straight into my front yard oak tree. I was the only person sober enough to think through the implications. I ran for my garden hose, which was in the back yard. By the time I reached the front yard again, I could see that the tree was on fire and that nobody had noticed.

I stumbled with the extra long hose to the front yard spigot. I screwed the hose on quickly and received a shower of cold water for my efforts. I hadn't tightened it enough. Never mind. I reeled around and shot a limp spray up at the tree but my hose wasn't strong enough. I dropped it and ran into my house to phone the fire department.

Back outside, I found Marcy and held her hand while most of the party stood and watched the upper limbs of my tree light up. Sparks were flying everywhere. I worried about my house. The firefighters arrived in minutes to spray the tree and my roof and the front of my house. They got the fire put out but not before the cracked front window gave way and gallons of water streamed into my living room. I sogged my way over through the wet grass to take a look through the window as the firefighters put away their gear. My furniture was ruined. And so were the walls. Peels of paint sloughed off the walls exposing the various shades of green they'd been painted this past year. I couldn't look any further. I stood there in the front yard with the fire truck lights behind me making my wet dress nearly invisible. But it didn't matter. My guests were streaming away down the street.

Constance, the last out of the driveway, turned around and waved a drink at me. "Come on, Jan, Grace said we could move the party to her house."

Sure enough, the lights had come on in Grace's house. Music was already blaring out the front door as revelers made their way into her house. Blinking water from my eyes, I focused on the people remaining in my yard. My mom, the Lois woman, and Margaret were scurrying around picking up trash, minding Marcy, and discussing logistics with the fire fighters. Jeff pulled up only moments later. I never responded to Constance who then shrugged and led her family off down to Grace's house.

Margaret took Marcy by the hand and led her inside. Jeff found a spare golf shirt in his car and slipped it over my head. It hung to my thighs, providing a modicum of decency. I inexplicably warmed at the sight of Jeff's car dealership logo on the front.

"What brought you here?"

"Marcy called me on my cell phone. The number must still be on your speed dial. She was upset and said that there was some sort of emergency so I came right over. Something about whales and poison apples, and party guests eating meat instead of vegetables." Jeff smiled. "But what brought me over was her comment that Mommy was 'sad, sad, sad.'"

"She said that?"

"She did. Very astute, that kid. Quite the prodigy."

I was quiet as I wondered what Marcy had been thinking. Jeff went over and dealt with the fire department, which departed shortly thereafter. I hugged my arms around Jeff's shirt. I didn't feel naked anymore.

Mule Slides pulled up a moment later. Apparently Marcy had run down all the speed dial numbers. As Jeff went over to deal with his mom, I wondered if Pizza Kitchen would be showing up soon to deliver a pizza. Close. A rental van pulled up and a representative (repo man?) for Kitchen Wonderful informed me that he was there to repossess the oven-fridge and dual drawer dishwasher. *Perfect.*

I sat down on my front step and cried. I didn't squirm away when Jeff sat down beside me and wrapped his arms around me. I just cried harder.

PART IV: DENOUEMENT

(Janice tidies up.)

YOU'RE INVITED

TO: A Get Acquainted Brunch

WHERE: Janice Darcy's House

WHEN: Wednesday, December 4
                        10:00 am

BRING: An Appetite!

RSVP: 555-6871

55. New Neighbors

I descended the stairs with Marcy on my tail. It was only eight o'clock but I was already dressed for the little brunch I was throwing for my new neighbors across the street. One of those home dry-cleaning concoctions had allowed me to wear my Lilly Pulitzer stuff far more often than the manufacturer had likely intended. I'd been wearing the same couple of outfits to pretty much everything lately. A simple sweater over my lime green top transformed the look for winter, although it was supposed to be seventy degrees this afternoon. *Once I get those credit card bills down a bit I'll work on the wardrobe situation.*

"Mommy?"

"What, Honey?" Marcy was still in her pajamas and probably wouldn't get dressed at all unless I got tough with her. Lately Marcy had been refusing to do anything for herself. The clothing thing had become an ongoing battle of wills, with me trying everything, including kiddy blackmail, to get Marcy to dress herself. Some days Marcy never got dressed at all. Not that it mattered. Marcy had done the impossible and flunked preschool.

More correctly, Marcy had been asked to come back after she got some counseling. As it turns out, other little kids get distracted when someone in their class spends the entire morning pretending to rid the classroom of monsters. The whole exorcist thing had begun after Mule Slides had shown Marcy *The Wizard of Oz*, or, as Marcy called it, The Famous Kids Movie. Now the only thing she would wear on her feet were a pair of sparkly red shoes we'd found at Target. They made her feel safe. And she wouldn't go to bed without clearing the closets of flying monkeys and green witches. The counselor had said that a lot of her behavior was age appropriate. But Marcy had clearly suffered from her parents' separation this past year.

"Mommy, is Nana up?"

"I don't know. Why don't you look in her room? She's going to play with you while Mommy has a few friends over to meet Mrs. Gordon."

The Gordons had moved into the Sturch's old house right after Halloween. The Sturches had sold and moved into an apartment during construction. Marcy and I had greeted the Gordons with cookies and found out that they had moved to Tampa from Manhattan. I had insisted on giving the fellow New Yorkers a little welcome-to-the-neighborhood brunch. I passed by my front window on the way to the kitchen and glanced over towards the Gordon's house.

"Marcy," I yelled back up the stairs. "Nana's out front. You can go talk to her if you put on some clothes."

"Is *Nana* dressed?"

Why such a smart child? "Sort of." My mother was standing out near the street talking to Mrs. Gordon in a muumuu. She had the newspaper in her hand. Mrs. Gordon was gesturing towards her driveway. Most likely, she was asking my mother for a solution to the oil stain that had plagued the driveway since the days of the Twin Vans.

In the eleven months since my mother had moved in, I had never felt more popular. The cruel joke, of course, was that everybody in my neighborhood was dropping by to visit my mother, not me. She had taken to practicing her tai chi in the front yard so that she could greet neighbors and dispense cleaning tips, her history as a janitor making her quite knowledgeable on the subject. My neighbors brought her tea and fruit salad and gushed to me about her incessantly whenever I ran into them at the grocery store.

"Which mop would your mom use on hardwood?"

"Does your mother use those electrostatic wipes?"

"Your mother told me to use bleach on the patio – does it matter if it's lemon-scented?"

"Where have you been hiding her all this time?"

"Ah ha! She's not dressed." Marcy opened the front door and ran out.

"Tell her that, would you?" I mumbled to myself as I went into the kitchen. It was sparkling clean and the coffee was already made. There certainly were a few perks to having a retired janitor living with you. The biggest advantage was that mom's pension money contributed to the mortgage, allowing all of us to stay put while I looked for a job. And I was getting used to driving up to the house and finding my mom in some strange contortion on the grass. Soon enough she would be moving to an apartment. Kate was now living full time in Clearwater with Gus. I rarely saw her but my mom never missed hearing Kate sing with Gus when the bar she worked at let them go on stage after Gus's band had finished for the night.

I had been dragging my heels a bit on the employment front. Necessary evils are still evil. But Jeff had demanded as part of our marriage counseling that I get a job to pay off the pile of debt I'd accumulated over the past year. He had moved back into our house but he wouldn't discuss moving my mother out until I was employed somewhere. So, I had done the unthinkable. I'd called Margaret. My interview at Sears was this afternoon. *Ugh*. I knew I was lucky that Margaret was even speaking to me, let alone hiring me. But it was still painful to contemplate. I poured myself a cup of coffee and started preparing food for the brunch: bagels, cheese, fruit salad, and chocolate éclairs.

My guests arrived just before ten. Jeff's mother came first. "Janice, Dear, do you have any water crackers?" Mule Slides asked. She positioned herself uncomfortably on a small side chair near the window. She placed the entire cheese plate in her lap and sniffed at the large cracker assortment on the table beside her. No water crackers. Her visits were infrequent but at least she would come inside the house now. Like everybody else, she sought out the cleaning advice of my mother. Mule Slides even snatched Mom out of the yard and dragged her over to her own house on occasion.

The rest of the neighbors arrived promptly, except Grace who had never responded to the invitation. Our friendship had cooled since the party on the Fourth. But everybody else came and as soon as they were settled, my new neighbor, Jody Gordon, regaled us all with stories about Manhattan and the sophisticated lifestyle she'd left behind due to her husband's transfer to Tampa. Wasn't Tampa such a funny, provincial little town? She just didn't know if she'd ever get used to it. Chuckle, chuckle. Jody stopped long enough to pull out a lipstick: Urban Decay.

Chuckle, chuckle, indeed. I felt a little defensive of my town. I wanted to say something but Jody Gordon was too quick and verbose.

"Of course, we're only living in this house until we have our new one built. We've already put a contract on a lot in New Suburb. There's a teardown on the lot but otherwise it's perfect. Everyone in my husband's office recommended New Suburb or Hyde Park. I guess everybody wants to be east of Dale Mabry."

What? Even I hadn't heard that one before. South of Kennedy, yes, but east of Dale Mabry? I scooted a little closer to Jody while the rest of the party digested the fact that this Jody-come-lately, for whom the party was for, felt that they all lived in an undesirable neighborhood.

"Jody," I inquired, "could I try that lipstick?" Jody handed it over. "Interesting brand. I'll bet you have tons of great clothes."

"I do. New York's great." Jody sighed. "You should come over sometime and check out my closet."

"I'd love to!" For a moment I envisioned the two of us jetting off to New York on a shopping spree. I didn't notice that several of my other guests were standing up, preparing to depart. I only noticed that everybody was paying attention when Jody Gordon responded.

"I'll make a pile and you can take whatever you like. Thanks. You've just saved me a trip to the Goodwill. Say, my friend Cathy is coming for a little dinner thing at my house tonight. Maybe she could bring some of her old clothes too. She was just telling me how she's got scads of last year's stuff clogging up her closet." Jody glanced out the front window as Marcy and her grandmother leapfrogged by. "Do you think your mom might like to earn a few extra dollars? We were all just saying that we could use a good housekeeper."

There was that "we" again. I suddenly felt myself transported back to Polly Hanson's front door on Halloween. I was all dressed up. The right people were there and I was invited. But I wasn't really in. And after nearly twenty-five years, I wasn't any closer.

Only this time, I really didn't care.

"Sorry, Jody. *We* can't spare her." We. My family. My friends. The only "we" that had ever mattered.

READER'S GUIDE

1.   Why does Janice Darcy try so hard to fit "in"? How did her upbringing affect her adult decision-making?

2.   Janice's "advice" is inane. Does she have any depth at all? Is Janice a good mother to Marcy?

3.   Discuss the parallels between Janice's constant upgrading of her living room paint and her make-up. Why does she do it?

4.   Why is Janice so frustrated with Jeff? with Kate?

5.   How can Janice, or anyone, balance too much self-esteem with too little?

6.   Discuss the tree motif and don't forget Janice's best friend, Margaret Oaks.

7.   How did Janice's relationship with Grace mirror her junior high school experiences?

8.   People normally want to feel a sense of belonging -- to family, to church, to their neighborhood, whatever. A lack of that sense can lead to senseless behavior. What did you think were Janice's funniest moments?

9.   Are there any similarities between Janice and the character, Madame Bovary?

Wendy Boucher is an author, artist and travel writer
residing in Tampa, Florida.

Order more copies of *Parvenue Throws A Party*
from Hoyden Press, LLC at
www.HoydenPress.com